MW01599563

The Last Frontier

of the Fading West

By Helen Picca

To Cory

Who made it possible for me to write this book. You gave me the place and the space, and the encouragement, to be able to weave the story I was inspired to write.

Prologue

I was clearing dishes from the early morning breakfast crowd when I saw the headline on the local paper, "Japanese Bomber to Visit Brookings." Seems the man responsible for dropping a bomb during the war on the forest outside of Brookings had been invited to the Azalea Festival there, 20 years later, as a gesture of peace. The war. That brought back a flood of memories that I hadn't thought about in a very long time.

I remember it like it was yesterday—the chaos, the fear, the uncertainty. . .the first time I saw him. The immediate attraction. That queasy, sort of stomach-turning sensation that set me all aflutter. I was young—so young—naïve, isolated in a small world of safety and comfort too soon shattered by a phone call. It was late at night. I was ready for bed, ready to climb between the covers to feel warm and sheltered. It was the doctor calling. There was an emergency—could I come help. A ship had sunk; many men were hurt. "Please come quickly" and the phone went dead. I stood there in a state of shock for what seemed like minutes but was, in fact, only moments. I tore off my night shirt and dressed quickly, putting on my uniform. There was a knock on my door. It was Pa wanting to know who was calling so late. I told him quickly what I knew as I put on my shoes. Could he drive me down to the Legion Hall where the survivors were being taken? We grabbed our coats and were off, rumbling down the hill in the old truck. My mind was racing. Never had there been such an emergency here in sleepy little Port Orford. Yes, ships had foundered and sunk—it was the Oregon coast. But never were there survivors brought to shore here, not in my lifetime.

I remembered how difficult that time was, the uneasiness that permeated the lives of everyone in this town— everyone along the coast. Now, thankful to be living without fear, I went back to my customers.

Port Orford 1942

These were strange and scary times. On December 7 of last year, my life, all our lives, changed. Gone were the carefree days of going to school or work, thinking about the dances coming up at the Grange, whether Tom would ask me out to a movie or for a soda at the fountain, the new fabric at the dry goods store and what pretty dresses Jane and I could make. Silly stuff really, but that's what young girls think about—those of us who live small lives, who've never left Port Orford, never been to a city like Portland. The safety and security of this small community of loggers and fishermen is all I've ever known. I'm only 18 and know so little about life and the world; I live safely at home with my Pa and my brother Frank. I have never even had to think about safety, I have always been safe and secure. We always had food, though sometimes not enough. Pa always took care of us even after Mama died. I never had to think about my wellbeing until that day.

Now I can hardly remember a time when I haven't been scared. Every day we hear news of shelling on the Oregon coast by the Japanese, like up at Ft. Stevens. Or the bomb that was dropped down in Brookings last month or sightings of these underwater ships called submarines. There was even an oil tanker sunk by one of them close to here, off Coos Bay. We've been living in the dark for months with blackout curtains over our windows at night and forbidden to be on the beach after dark. Much of the time there has been no gas for the truck, no kerosene for the lamps, no sugar, no coffee—all those supplies going to support our troops now that we were at war. I didn't mind those sacrifices knowing my brother was now one of them. He'd joined the Coast Guard shortly after Pearl Harbor was attacked and he was another thing that I had to worry about. I was so scared he would be hurt or worse yet, killed. Ships were being shelled and sunk all over the Pacific, though I had no idea where he was. I held my breath between letters from him and prayed I would never see the Western Union man in our drive.

There was lots of news coming out of Washington, but about actual battles, the news was spotty—very little was printed in the newspaper here. Much of what we did learn was hearsay from people passing through, or from letters our neighbors got. We heard a story of a Coast Guard cutter bombing a German submarine off Cape Hatteras, somewhere on the east coast. The submarine surfaced and gunners fired on the crew as they tried to escape. Then the cutter, I think the name was *Icarus*, rammed the sub and sunk it. The person telling the story didn't know what happened to the survivors. I wondered if maybe my brother was on that cutter—could he be patrolling U.S. coastlines and us not know it? And now a ship was sunk right here where we live. Could it have foundered on some rocks like so many ships before it? Like the *Cottoneva* that ran aground right here by Battle Rock. No, there's been no storm. It's been clear and the sea has been calm. All of this has been rambling through my brain as we drove here to the hall in the dark with the lights out—thankfully there was moonlight tonight. But now we are here and there is chaos, people running in and out with boxes and blankets. There's Dr. Griffin. Pa parked the truck and we ran to him.

"Thank God you're here," he said to me then turned to Pa. "James, you can help too. Go inside and help set up the cots." He took hold of my elbow, "You come with me and we'll just see what we are up against."

I was quite a bit in shock, but I went with him into the hall. There were about 20 men in various states, all bedraggled, dirty, wet and cold. I saw blood and smelled something horrible—burned flesh. My stomach clenched. I wanted to turn around and run out the door, but something gripped me and forced me to remember this was what I had been training to do. I had been working at Doc's office for over a year now, since graduating high school, assisting him, learning from him how to treat cuts, scrapes, gashes, broken bones. But never had there been so many all at once, it was always one at a time. Men were moaning. Someone was calling my name. I felt dazed. "Jennifer." It was Doc Griffin. I turned to look at him and was snapped back to reality. "You start here and evaluate their wounds. Any that seem superficial that need cleaning and bandaging, go ahead and take care of them. Any that seem more serious, you send to me, OK?" I nodded and barely said okay and he was off to the other side of the room where men were laying on cots and not moving.

The first man I saw had blood dripping down his face onto his legs. I instantly dropped into action. I ran to the table where supplies had been set up and grabbed some gauze, saline and iodine and ran back to him. I made him lie down to lessen the blood flow and applied some gauze pads with pressure to stop it altogether. He seemed to be in shock but looked into my eyes. "You're alright," I said. "You're alright now. Just a cut. You'll be fine." As I spoke to him with a forced smile and gently cleaned his wound, he seemed to relax. He had a small gash on his forehead. I swabbed it in iodine, covered it with gauze, wrapped a bandage around his head and tied it gently in place.

I patted his shoulder and told him to rest. I would come back to check on him. I moved on to the next man.

*

When I finished the last man, I went back through them. They were all resting with no visible signs of bleeding. There were 18 of them. I realized someone had separated them. These men had superficial injuries, though some of them had multiple wounds. These were the cases I could handle, cuts and gashes that needed to be cleaned and bandaged, nothing life-threatening. Seeing them resting quietly, I felt a wave of exhaustion and decided to go outside for some cool night air. The air was cool, but it was no longer night, dawn was breaking—I had no idea so much time had passed and suddenly felt even more tired. I wanted to go home and climb into my safe, warm bed and sleep for days. I wanted to go back to yesterday morning, when the day loomed before me with a promise of routine and thoughts of Tom.

"How are you doing?" My reverie was broken by Doc.

"I'm fine. Just getting some air."

"I checked your patients," he said with a smile. "You did a fine job."

I was thrilled that he had said "your patients" and filled with pride. "Thank you, I just used what I learned from you."

"Yes, but you never had to handle more than one patient and this was quite overwhelming. You didn't panic. Just dug in and got to work. You'll make a fine nurse."

"It was a bit overwhelming with so many. Do you know what happened to them?"

"Yes. Commander Wilson came down from the Coast Guard Station to check on how many men we had here and what condition they were in. He said they were torpedoed, presumably by a Japanese submarine."

"Oh, no." Tears filled my eyes and all the fears I felt over the last year rose up inside of me. "Will they attack us?"

"No, no, don't worry." He put his arm around my shoulder to comfort me like my father would do. "Wilson says there's no sign of them anywhere along the coast. He's been in touch with the other stations. He's also been in touch with the Navy."

"The Navy? Are our ships out there?" I asked.

"Well there probably are, but he was reporting on the six Navy crew that were on that tanker."

I wasn't aware that any of these men were Navy, I hadn't seen any uniforms. "Oh, are they okay?" I asked.

"Those are the men I've been treating. . .the three of them that survived. And they're pretty badly burned." He turned solemn and looked off toward the ocean.

It was then I remembered that smell and tried to imagine what they would look like. I'd never seen burned flesh before.

"I was hoping you could help me with the last man. He's not too badly burned and you could learn how to treat a burn," he said.

I was hesitant. I didn't want to have an image like that in my head for the rest of my life. But if I really did want to be a nurse, I would need to confront the worst of the worst. And Doc said the burns weren't too bad. Before I could think any more about it and change my mind, I said, "Yes, of course." And that moment would change my life forever.

We went back into the hall to the rear where privacy screens had been set up. Doc led me into one partitioned cubicle where there was a man on a table. He was undressed except for a sheet wrapped around his midriff. He had burns on his legs, chest and arms. They looked bad but were not horrifying, though the smell was harder to handle. Doc handed me a surgical mask and a pair of rubber gloves.

"Put these on and we'll get started. I've given him morphine so he won't feel anything."

I did as I was told. Doc showed me how to swab the burns with gauze soaked in saline in an attempt to remove any of the loose burned skin. It was a slow process and we went through so many gauze swabs.

At one point, the man flinched and yelled, scaring the wits out of me. I jumped and gasped and we stopped what we were doing. In a few seconds, he was quiet again but for the first time I was looking at his face. He was handsome with a broad, square, tanned face. His hair was brown but blond on top like a man who spent a lot of time in the sun. I wondered about his eyes—what color they were. His lips were chapped from exposure to the salt, but held my gaze. I felt this incredible urge to touch them.

I heard Doc saying, "He might be reliving the trauma subconsciously. Let's keep going. I want to finish before the sedation wears off."

So, we proceeded to remove whatever loose skin and debris would come off easily. Not wanting to exert too much pressure and cause him any more pain, we cleaned as best we could the layer of oil that still coated his body. It was tedious work but eventually, we had cleaned each burn area and applied a topical solution Doc said was best for burns—I think it was tannic acid. That combined with the penicillin shot Doc gave him should keep infection away and let him heal.

"That should do him for a while," Doc said resolutely, then turned to me. "I want you, young lady, to go home and get some sleep. Later on, you can come back and help me reapply the solution to these men."

I didn't need much convincing; I was dog-tired. "All right, but what about you?" I asked.

"Don't worry about me. I'll grab a few hours on that cot over there." He paused and then added, "You were a great help to me, Jennifer, I'm not sure I could have handled this alone."

"I'm so glad I could help. I learned a lot tonight. Not only about medicine but about myself. I mean, about seeing all this blood and torn flesh. I guess I will be able to handle being a nurse."

"You will. There's no doubt in my mind. You came through this tonight without hesitation and really helped save lives. Those men out there think you walk on water for the gentle care you gave them," he said as he chuckled. "You made them feel safe and like they were getting special care. That's the most important part of being a nurse."

"Well, you didn't see it, but I did hesitate at first. But once I got started, it all felt so easy and natural. I liked it. I liked helping them a lot."

"Good. Now go find your Pa and go home. And I'll see you later."

He gave me a hug and off I went. Doc was like a father to me. I remember him coming to our house when I was a little girl with chicken pox. He came into my room and was so kind and funny. I asked him where I got *chicken pops* from and he said, "From chickens, silly." I liked him instantly. He's cared for our whole family over the years, just like all the other families in this town, and he spent a lot of time with me when my mother was so sick. I had nursed her when she was too sick to get out of bed. He saw my interest in medicine, and taught me and encouraged me. When I graduated from high school, he took me on as an assistant. I would do anything I could for him and wouldn't let him down.

I found Pa in the kitchen drinking coffee and talking with other men from town. Jim Dyer was talking about the incident. I heard him say he was on the beach when they brought the survivors in. He helped get the men out of the lifeboats and drove as many as would fit in his truck up here. He started to say something about wanting to wretch, but saw me and stopped talking. Pa got up and came to me, put his arms around me and held me tight, his chin on the top of my head.

"Are you done?" he asked.

"Yes. Doc told me to go home and sleep and come back later. Can you take me home?" I asked.

"Of course. Let's go." He turned back to the men and said, "Gonna take my girl home. I'll see you all later." And with that, we left the hall.

We drove home in silence, both too tired to speak. We'd been up over 24 hours. We pulled in the drive and parked at the door, Pa stopped and shut off the truck. He took hold of my hand and squeezed it and said "Jenny, I just want you to know how very proud I am of you." He was looking straight ahead, not at me. I knew how hard it was for him to express any kind of emotion.

I squeezed his hand back and said, "I know Pa. And your telling me makes me feel proud and happy you're my Pa."

Pa nodded, let go of my hand and said, "Now let's both go get some sleep."

*

We got back to the hall around five that night, having gotten about six hours sleep. I felt like a shadow of myself, not entirely there. When I'd gotten home this morning, I remember stripping off my dirty, bloody clothes and climbing under the covers. I think I was asleep when my head hit the pillow. I woke up to my stomach growling and realized I hadn't eaten since the prior night's dinner. I got up, washed and dressed in an old dress—I only had the one uniform I'd worn the day before. I fixed Pa and myself some food and off we were again, rumbling down the road.

The men I'd treated last night were mostly in the kitchen eating or drinking coffee, some still laying on their cots. There were some women from the Red Cross there cooking and serving the men. One of the men called to me as I came in. I went to his table where he was sitting with a few other men.

"What is your name?" he asked.

"Jenny," I replied.

"Well, nurse Jenny, I just want to thank you for your kindness last night. You patched me up and made me not be afraid and I am grateful." The others chimed in their agreement and echoed his thanks. "We are all grateful," he finally said.

"I am so happy to see you all up and moving around. And eating. I was happy to do what I could for you. Are you feeling okay?"

"Yes, yes. A little sore but happy to be alive." The others were shaking their heads in agreement. One said, "Amen, brother."

"Well, if you need anything from me, let me know. I'm going to check on the other patients," I said as I moved into the hall. I walked to the back of the room and there was Doc, looking exhausted, but working tirelessly on one of the burn victims.

"Ah, Jenny. I'm glad you're here."

I felt so sorry for him. He needed—and probably wanted—sleep badly but his sense of duty and his oath wouldn't let him stay away from his patients.

"Doc, show me what to do and go get some sleep," I said.

"No, I'm fine. But you can help me. We need to keep applying this solution to the burns every couple of hours. I've finished these two men, but the last one needs to be done."

"Okay. I can do that. Just like you are doing. But please go get some sleep. You are no good to anyone if you keel over."

He was about to respond, to reject that idea, so I grabbed the swab from his hand and pushed him in the direction of the cot in the back hallway. He sighed and relented, knowing I was right. He patted me on the shoulder and walked away.

I put on some gloves and a mask and resumed his work. He seemed to have placed the men in the order of most burned to least, so the last man was not the worst case I had to look upon. In fact, he was the best to look upon, the handsome man I had helped Doc with last night. I looked at the notes Doc was keeping on each man, his name was Jack Long. I proceeded to treat his burns, though I confess, I looked quite often at his face and his torso which was tall, lean and quite muscular. With a stab of embarrassment, I realized I was enjoying swabbing his wounds far more than the other men. He was still sedated, like the others, so I still couldn't see his eyes, but I felt something different with him. I sensed his spirit, a kindness, a tenderness or something I couldn't quite explain. As I worked on him, I sat there mesmerized by that feeling for I am not sure how long. I was just finishing up on the last burn when I heard my name being called. It was the man I spoke with in the kitchen, a man called Pat. He was calling me to come to where the other patients were. Several men were holding down another on the cot and I could see blood through the bandages.

"He was thrashing around like he was having a nightmare and must have opened up his wounds," Pat said.

He was awake now and looking quite scared. He was young—no more than my age. I sat next to him and touched his forehead; he seemed to relax right away. "It's alright, you're going to be alright," I said as cheerily as I could muster. I took hold of his arm which was now covered in a bloody bandage. I used scissors to cut it free to see what was happening. It looked okay, no sign of any infection, just reopened and bleeding again. I placed some gauze on it and held it tight and slightly elevated to get it to stop. He was looking alarmed, so I patted his shoulder and told him it was nothing, that I would just re-bandage it and it would be fine so long as he stopped swatting flies. He laughed a little and I proceeded to swab it with iodine and re-bandage it with a few extra layers, just in case.

He thanked me and I smiled at him hoping to make him feel safe. I checked on a few of the other men still in their cots and all seemed well, just in need of a little attention.

I realized a couple of hours had passed and with Doc nowhere in sight, I went back to the burn victims and started with the first patient. Doc hadn't lied. This man was very badly burned, which made me realize how much he needed my best care and total dedication. I went to work.

*

The next day when I arrived, the men with the cuts and gashes were gone. The company that owned the tanker had sent a bus to transport them to Portland for further treatment and release or redeployment on another ship. There were many ships moving goods up and down the coast to Portland and San Francisco where the cargo was reloaded onto supply ships for our troops in the Pacific. But being on a merchant ship was not the safest place to be, many ships were being attacked in both the Pacific and the Atlantic.

I had learned from the men I treated that their ship was an oil tanker called the *Larry Doheny* en route to Portland. There had been 46 men on board, six of which were Navy men there to defend the ship. There had been a big explosion during the night that rocked the ship, which they came to discover was a torpedo from a submarine. The boat was taking on water, so the crew lowered the lifeboats and left the ship. The Navy men stayed on board at the gun waiting for the submarine to surface, to strike a blow, but then the ship caught fire and with all that oil, the ship and the sea around it became an inferno. They jumped overboard, along with the captain—that's how they got burned. Three of the men and the captain never resurfaced.

They said it was eerie to think the enemy was beneath the water, stalking them, never making their presence known. Some of the men said they wouldn't go back to the sea, they'd go find work in an airplane factory or shipyard where there was a shortage of labor.

It was hard for me to imagine what these men had been through and were continuing to struggle with. Many of them had worked on ships, been at sea, their whole lives. Some had families relying on them, but the threat of more serious injury (like the burned Navy men) or death, was about to deprive them of their chosen livelihood.

With the bulk of the men gone, it was much quieter here in the hall. The remaining three men were healing, though they had a long way to go. We still needed to treat the wounds with the solution, but not as often. Doc was backing off on the morphine, as well, for the two less-severely burned. He and I worked out a schedule so we could each get some decent sleep and it was now my shift. I was to treat all three men and then was free to go, which I was anxious to do. I realized this morning that there was a dance at Rainbow Gardens this Saturday and my dress was only half finished. I needed time to work on that.

The first man was pretty much the same as he had been yesterday, completely sedated. I took my time, gently swabbing each burn. It was remarkable to me how quickly I had grown accustomed to the seared flesh, both the sight and the smell. I didn't flinch, though it was quite horrid looking, and almost mechanically moved from burn to burn. I could tell the last two men were less sedated, as now and then, they would flinch when I touched a particularly bad area. When I got to Jack, he moaned as I swabbed his shin which had a pretty serious burn on it. I stopped and looked at his face. His eyes were still closed, but his brow was furrowed. "Am I hurting you?" I asked, not really expecting to get an answer. There was no response, so I continued. Again, he moaned and I stopped. "Do you need something for the pain?" I asked. With still no response, I went back to swabbing. He moaned again, louder this time. I stopped again. "I only have a little more to do. Can you stand the pain?" Still no response. I went back to my work and was just about done, when he said, "Are you an angel?" I was surprised and not sure what to say or do. His eyes were still closed, so I guessed he was in a state somewhere between conscious and unconscious. "Yes," I said, "I am your angel of mercy here to heal you." He relaxed then and the corners of his lips turned slightly up into a smile, so I quickly finished up and let him rest peacefully.

*

I went home and tried to focus on finishing the dress I was making for the dance Saturday night, and wishing Jane was here to help me get it done. It was hard to think about having fun when there was so much death and destruction all around us. Hard to get rid of the uneasy feeling I had day after day, what with ships being sunk and Ft. Stevens being shelled. . .that was only 300 miles away, right on the coast, just like us. We heard more details about Brookings, just south of us, being bombed. Then, there was a small fire in the forest just east of us and rumor had it there was a small plane flying over at about the same time. Thankfully, all the rain we'd had quashed that fire before it could spread. Being on the coast, we were vulnerable and the Japanese seemed to be vicious, horrible people who would stop at nothing to kill us all.

I forced myself to think about Saturday night and the hope that Tom would ask me to dance. Even that didn't set my mind at ease—he could be drafted at any moment. The dress was almost finished, it just needed to be hemmed and the facings tacked; then I would iron it and it would be ready to wear. It would be ever so much prettier with silk stockings, but, of course, there were none of those to be had. Socks would have to do. At least I wouldn't be the only one wearing them.

Before I knew it, it was time to be getting back to the hall. I would have to walk as Pa was working at the mine. That was one good thing that came out of this war. Like so many previously unemployed Americans, Pa had work again. After the closing of the mill where he worked, he had trouble finding steady work, but now they were mining chromium, which the government needed for making steel. The work was steady and the pay good.

Just as I got to the hall, Doc was rushing out. Said he'd had an emergency call at his office and would be back as soon as possible. I asked if I could help him and he said yes, "Take care of the men. Continue the treatments like you've been doing." And with that, he was off. So, I went in and went through the routine again from worst to best case. Nothing much different than when I was here this morning. I was finishing up on Jack Long, that nasty burn on his leg, when he flinched and sucked in his breath. That burn was pretty severe and I knew it must be painful.

"Am I burned badly?" he asked.

Surprised that he was awake, I pulled back and looked at his face. His eyes were open and he was looking right at me. I didn't know what to say, this was the first time any of these men had consciously spoken to me. I told him it was okay, that he would be okay.

"Tell me," he said, more forcefully.

I could sense he was agitated, understandably, having woken up in pain, in a strange place, with a stranger prodding his hurt, so I chose my words carefully. "Well, you have some minor burns on your arms and chest. They've healed quite a bit since you got here. This burn on your leg is worse, but it is better. And will heal. All your burns will heal. You'll be good as new." I said this trying to smile, to lay his fears to rest.

"Then why does it hurt so much? Why does it feel like someone is stabbing me over and over again?"

"Well, the tissue is still. . ." I stopped, realizing that saying anything detailed about the burn would be too graphic for him. So instead, I said, "Your injuries are only two days old, and we have to keep swabbing them to promote healing. And you are healing. In another day or two you'll be able to walk out of here."

"Where is here?" he asked.

"You are in the Legion Hall of Port Orford."

"In California?"

"No, you're in Oregon, southern Oregon," I clarified.

"What about the others, the rest of my gun crew?"

"There are three of you here. All of you were burned when you jumped from the ship." He had lots of questions about the rest of the crew, the captain, the ship, which I answered as best I could, knowing it was difficult for him to hear. He asked if we got the submarine, but I told him I hadn't heard anything about that.

Then he asked if I was the angel he had seen. I laughed and said I was no angel, but that I'd been here since he was brought in, helping Doc as best I could to treat their wounds. I realized I was staring at him, at his eyes, which I was seeing for the first time. They were blue, the most beautiful shade of blue I had ever seen. They were warm and kind and seemed to penetrate right through me. They seemed to be smiling at me.

"What's your name?" he wanted to know.

"Jenny," I said.

"How is it that someone so young knows so much about treating burns?" he asked.

"Honestly. . . I just learned. I've been working with the Doctor here in town for about two years, part time at first, after school, learning about first aid. But until two nights ago, had never seen or treated a burn before. Doc showed me what to do and I've been doing it just like he said ever since."

"You have a very gentle hand," which I was glad to hear since I had thought, at times, I had been hurting him.

I smiled at him and then, trying to keep his mind off his wounds said, "Tell me about Jack Long. How did you come to be on that ship?"

He proceeded to tell me he was from Los Angeles and had enlisted a year ago, just before Pearl Harbor, and explained what it was like to be in the Navy. He told me he was an only child and that his parents had died in a car accident just before he enlisted. He asked about my family and I told him about my Mama and Pa and my brother Frank in the Coast Guard on a ship somewhere. He asked about Port Orford, if it had any claim to fame. "You mean you've never heard of Port Orford?" I asked jokingly. I would have been very surprised if anyone from Los Angeles had heard of such a small town on the Oregon Coast; we were just a speck on the edge. I went on to tell him about our trees, the Port Orford Cedar—how unique and prized the wood was—about our being the only deep-water harbor within a thousand miles on the West Coast, about the Coast Guard station, about the saw mill and the mining. I told him we were the oldest incorporated town on the West Coast, and how the town got its start after a fight with the Indians at Battle Rock. I even told him how our former mayor tried to get the southern Oregon and northern California counties to secede and create the 49th state of Jackson. He was amazed that there was so much happening here and he'd never heard of it. We talked for several hours; he was easy to talk to, and very pleasant to look at, especially those beautiful blue eyes. I felt a connection to him, an excitement that I'd never felt before.

I heard footsteps behind me and turned to see Doc coming my way. He was back. I excused myself from Jack and went to see Doc to report on the condition of the men and in particular, Jack.

Before I could say anything, Doc said, "Jenny, that emergency was Tom. He had an accident up at the logging camp and has lost a finger, I'm afraid." Doc knew I was sweet on Tom.

"Oh, no. Is he alright?" I asked, trying hard not to panic.

"Yes, he should be fine. I had to amputate his finger, though—his index finger. But he should heal up fine. We'll just have to keep it clean and make sure it doesn't get infected. You can help with that if you want."

"Yes, yes, of course," I sputtered. I knew full well that Tom would be fine. He was tough as nails, had been logging for three years, went into it right after graduation, just like his Pa. It was hard and dangerous work, and he'd had plenty of cuts, bruises and even broken bones. I also knew he would go back to work, that he would adapt—he had too much pride to do otherwise.

"Tom is home. Why don't you go visit him?" Doc said.

I was quick to leave and so anxious to see Tom to comfort him, but not before giving Doc a brief report on the men, especially Jack, who was now awake.

When I got to Tom's house, his mother let me in. She was visibly upset. "Oh, Jenny, I guess you heard about Tom." She had tears in her eyes. I gave her a hug and she hugged me back.

"Doc told me," I said. "He also told me Tom will heal and be fine."

"Yes, but his finger is gone," she said hysterically and burst into tears, pointed to the living room and ran away, down the hall.

I turned and rushed in. Tom was seated in an upholstered chair with his arm propped up on a pillow. His hand was bandaged to almost twice its normal size and there was an ice bag on top. He was looking at me and trying to smile, but I could tell he was in a lot of pain. "Hi, Jenny," he managed to say.

I ran over and knelt on the floor beside him and gently touched his upper arm. I gulped down my anxiety and tried to act calm, even though the sight of him was quite upsetting. "Hi, Tom. Doc told me what happened. I'm so sorry," trying to console him. "Did Doc give you anything for the pain?" I asked.

"He gave me a shot, but it's starting to wear off," he winced as he said it. "But I'll be alright, no need to worry about me." I could tell he was acting brave and strong for my benefit.

"I know," I said as I touched his cheek. "Is there anything I can do for you or get for you?" I offered, knowing as I said it, there was little I could do. All he needed was time.

"No, no. It's getting late, it will be dark soon. Why don't you head home?" He paused and looked at his hand. "You know, it would mean a lot to me if you could go with me tomorrow back to Doc's. He wants to check it, make sure there's no infection."

"Of course, what time do you have to go?"

"He said in the afternoon, around 4 o'clock."

"Okay, I'll come by at 3:30 and we can walk over."

Port Orford was such a small town, if you lived within city limits, you could walk to everything. All the shops and services were along the main street and we all lived off of that.

I gave his other hand a squeeze and rose to leave. "I'll see you then. Try to get some sleep and be sure to keep ice on it. That will help with the pain."

"Okay," he said as he squeezed my hand back. I left without saying goodbye to Mrs. Flynn, who never reappeared.

Walking home, I was chilled to the bone. I had worn only a light jacket when I left earlier today and now the wind was howling, and the temperature had dropped. Another storm was rolling in. I hurried along to get home before it started to rain.

I made it to the house just in time. Once inside, I put on some flannel pajamas, wool socks and my warm robe and made a cup of tea. I sat there in the living room thinking about all that had happened today, letting the warm clothes and hot tea penetrate my insides as I watched the cold rain lash the window panes and the trees bend from the gale-force winds.

I was sitting on my sofa watching the storm. The rain was violently lashing against the windows that lined the side of the house facing the sea. The panes were flexing and the trees were swaying from the wind that was howling from the south. Clouds were so thick and low I could barely see the edge of the bluff, let alone the dock below.

I felt safe though, this house was rock solid, built almost 30 years ago of Port Orford Cedar. It was a historic place filled with many tales. It was built in 1935 as the administration building for Gilbert Gable's many enterprises, a large elaborate structure with three massive fireplaces and numerous rooms. Sometimes when I sit here alone, I can feel the energy and spirit of the place as he built it. He had come to this town filled with hopes of making this little hamlet a major port between San Francisco and Portland. He owned a lumber company, a gold mine, the wharf, a realty company, engineering firm and a railroad, which was nothing more than a wish he tried to make come true and failed. (He had petitioned the federal and state governments to build a railroad inland from this town to points east, all part of his plan to grow this little harbor into a major shipping port. He was a persistent and charming man, but was denied and died shortly thereafter—the dream of a railroad dying with him.) During the war, the Coast Guard used the property as a communications center for beach patrols with kennels for the canine unit they housed here.

After the war, the building was bought by a retired Army colonel who turned it into the Castaway Lodge, offering cocktails, fine dining and rooms for the night. The place was very successful and he accommodated visitors from all over the globe. Tom and I had our wedding here, our wedding photo taken right out there on the bluff with the ocean and southern coastline in the background. It was a beautiful, sunny day, not at all like today.

The Colonel sold the place a few years later and it went downhill from there. In 1958, it burned to the ground, purposely, for the insurance money. Unfortunately for the owner, he was found out and sent to prison along with his paid arsonist.

All that was left of the building was this east wing and the three river-rock chimneys standing sentinel. The current owner, who is a mystery man, renovated the standing wing into a small house, in which living room I sit today. No one knows much about him, including me. The few times he stayed here, he kept completely to himself. He's become part of the mystique of this town, just like the fog that shrouds our little municipality so often during the year.

After Tom died two years ago, Mr. Feldon, the town lawyer, came to see me, to help me sort out finances. Tom, characteristically, left no will, no life insurance and quite a few debts, none of which I knew about—he was not done making my life miserable. Mr. Feldon said I would have to sell the house just to cover the debts. This wasn't too much of a surprise; I was having trouble paying the water and electric bills, let alone the taxes, which were overdue. I was feeling panicky. Here I was with four children, very little money and now, no place to live. My eyes welled up. The stress and strain of the last two years was just too much. I wanted to curl up in a ball, and pull the world in around me.

"Jennifer, don't worry. It's all going to be alright. You have a job," he said.

I'd been working at CJ's ever since Tom died and made enough money to feed us and keep the kids in clothes and shoes. There wasn't much left over and whatever was left I stashed in the bank for those weeks that were slow.

"Yes, but I don't make that much. Really just enough to get by. I've been thinking of getting a second job, which I guess I will have to do to have money for rent now."

"Well, I figured as much. That's part of why I am here today," he said sympathetically.

I was visibly upset, tears were leaking down my cheeks, but I thought, maybe he had a job for me.

"I had a call from a lawyer in Los Angeles. His client owns the house on the bluff and is looking for someone to care-take it. Apparently, his work keeps him very busy and with all his travelling, he won't be able to get up here. He wants someone in there to make sure it's maintained and doesn't become a derelict property," he offered.

"But I can't maintain it. I can barely maintain this house," I said rejecting his generous offer.

"Don't worry. All the bills are paid by the owner. The lights, the water, the taxes. Your boys can take care of the grounds. There'll even be funds if something breaks and needs repair. You'll just be there to watch over the place. But it will be your home. The lawyer assured me you could stay as long as necessary."

I couldn't believe this was happening. They say when something sounds too good to be true, it usually is. I sat there in disbelief. Could I be so lucky? Could this be true?

But true it was. I'd been here over a year and loved the serenity of the place as did my kids. They seemed to be thriving without Tom to yell at them. . .and me.

There was a loud crack and I snapped back to reality. The wind and the rain were fierce—reminding me of that storm twenty years ago, when I was innocent and filled with hope and the promise for a happy future.

When I woke the next day, the wind and rain were beyond robust and I was filled with anxiety about getting to the hall to help Doc and then getting to Tom later in the day. This storm was a doozy. I got dressed, had some oatmeal, then put on my boots and slicker, ready to face the weather outside. I wasn't concerned so much with the rain, but the wind was pretty strong, rattling the windows; I knew it was going to be hard to walk. But at least it was coming from the south, so it would push me along.

I opened the front door and it nearly flew out of my hand—this was going to be tough. I managed to close the door and trudged out into it, keeping my head low. I was pushed and pulled and drowned with rain, but managed to get to the hall in one piece. I stepped inside feeling like a drowned rat. I was shaking off my hat and making a puddle on the floor when I saw Doc coming my way.

"Jenny. I just tried to call you. You're here early," he said hurriedly.

"I wanted to get here a little early so I could leave early to go with Tom to your office later. Why did you call?" I asked.

"I wanted to tell you not to bother coming here. The men are gone. They just left a little while ago."

"Gone? What do you mean? They weren't well enough to leave," I said in disbelief.

"The Navy sent a transport for them. Took them to Portland, to the hospital where they could get a better treatment for burns." Doc must have seen the look of confusion on my face and went on. "Apparently, there's a new method for treating burns developed in England using materials we don't have here. It's proven very effective. We did the best with what we had—you did all you could for them. Probably helped save them. You should feel good about that." Doc was thinking I was concerned about their wellbeing, when all I really cared about was seeing Jack.

"I just thought I'd have the chance to see them recover more. You know, come out of the sedation, like Jack," I said, trying to camouflage my real feelings.

"Yes, Jack. He thanked me for our work, told me to thank you. He called you his angel of mercy."

I stood there in my puddle, feeling soggy and sad.

"We're just wrapping up here. You can help me and then I'll drive you home," Doc offered.

"Alright," I managed to say. I took off my coat and went to work packing up the supplies, but feeling a big hole inside me. I realized how much I had been looking forward to talking more with Jack, to being near him. I laughed at myself to think about the romantic fantasies I had been conjuring of him. As much as I liked Tom and was worried about him, there was something special about Jack, a way he made me feel that I never felt with Tom. He was from someplace far away and had seen so much more of the world than me or Tom and he was only a little older. I wanted to know what it was like to grow up in a big city with so many people. I just wanted to know more about him and to look in his beautiful blue eyes.

Doc drove me home and before I got out of his car, he thanked me for all my help, said he couldn't have handled it without me. I smiled as best I could and nodded, afraid that if I spoke, the floodgates would open and all my sadness and disappointment would gush out. He said not to worry about Tom, he would stop on his way home and check his hand.

"Best be getting inside and be safe, and don't worry about coming to the office tomorrow. This storm is predicted to be bad," Doc said.

I thanked him for the ride home and got out of the car, using all my strength to push the door open. I trudged the short distance to the house, got quickly in and slammed the door, wondering how it could possibly be worse than this.

Port Orford 1962

Just when you think it can't get any worse, it usually does. I woke up early in the morning to the roaring sound of the wind. It was blowing like I'd never heard before. It was Columbus Day and I knew there was no way there would be a parade today. The kids would be disappointed, but right now I wanted to make sure they were safe. I'd never seen a gale like this. I'd lived here my whole life—38 years—and never seen a storm like this; the sound was deafening. I went to the boy's room and flipped the light switch, but nothing happened. The electric was out. "Mom, we can't sleep," my son said in the dark.

"It's okay, Jimmy, it's just a storm. You rest while I go check on your sisters."

I went back out into the living room and closed the drapes. I didn't want my kids to see what was happening outside—it was too scary. The trees were practically horizontal. For the first time, I was sorry to live out here on the bluff, so exposed to weather and sorry to have all those windows facing the storm. I ran to get my girls. At 9 and 11 they were scared and so impressionable. I put on a brave front so as not to scare them further and led them, with their pillows, to their brothers' room for a "storm shelter" I called it. I put the girls in one bed and the boys in the other and we sat there in the dark with the door closed and windows covered, with the sounds of the storm crashing all around us. The whole house was shaking from the intense wind. I could hear buildings being ripped apart and trees being torn from the ground and snapping like matchsticks. I proceeded to tell them stories that I knew about the town, about how Captain Tichenor came to start it, about the Indian encounter at Battle Rock, the myth of the 10-ton Port Orford meteorite, about Graveyard Point being dynamited to yield the rocks to create the dock, what the town was like when I was a little girl—anything I could think of to keep their minds occupied. I lit some candles and we ate cookies with milk, so it would seem more like a party than the life-threatening event it was.

I just kept telling them stories. Like about the early settlers who came by wagon from the east, often suffering starvation, broken axles and wheels, the constant threat of encountering hostile Indians, getting trapped in the uncharted mountains and canyons, and the hardships they had to endure once they got here. Not just the homesteaders, but the miners too, the men who came looking for gold, young men and boys who came from as far away as Illinois in search of riches that they never found. They had to deal with all sorts of weather, very often without hard shelter, but I wondered secretly if they ever encountered a storm such as this. For 12 hours, I listened to the wind blowing and the rain pounding on the roof and windows, heard the house groan as if it would rip apart, all the while praying that nothing would fall on the house or shatter a window, so anxious for it to end.

At long last, the winds died down and the rain let up. I opened a curtain and it seemed to be over. I went into the living room and opened the drapes one by one. The scene outside was surreal. Trees were down as far as I could see. There were boats flipped over on the wharf or blown completely off and crashed on the shore. There was lumber and all sorts of debris in the harbor. We could see into town, a view which had always been blocked by trees—they were all gone. I walked around the whole house, inside and out, and all seemed to be intact. There were no leaks, no apparent damage. There was plenty of debris in the yard, and all our trees were down, but we seemed to have come through the storm unscathed, though as I looked around, I knew that others weren't quite so lucky.

In the days that followed, we learned that it was a tropical storm from way out in the Pacific—one for the record books—that became known as the Columbus Day Storm of 1962. The winds at Cape Blanco were more than 145 mph, as high as their gauge went. Some said 170 mph. The town was in shambles. It looked like what I imagined a war zone would look like: fallen trees everywhere, including on many roofs, roofs completely ripped off, houses knocked off their foundations, many shattered windows, downed power lines. . .even the sea gulls seemed dazed. Miraculously, no one was hurt in our town. Oregon had been in the eye of the storm and most severely damaged, though northern California and Washington were affected as well.

As usual, the town came together to make do and get the town and its people put back together. As soon as folks felt safe enough to come out of their shelter, the recovery began. CJ, with his gas-powered grill and generator, served coffee and eggs to anyone who came by, free of charge. Men who owned chain saws drove around, clearing driveways and roadways that were blocked. It took almost two weeks to restore phone service to everyone. Crews from the electric company brought generators to the businesses that needed refrigeration, then worked doggedly to restore power—it was three days before the lights came back on in our house. We learned to do without, but were happy to share whatever we had. People pooled their resources and shared their homes with those less fortunate. I guess that's one of the many reasons I have always loved this town: Being so isolated, we take care of our own.

The events of the last few days had taken their toll on me. I did not go to the dance; I still felt deflated and sad. I visited Tom a few times to keep his spirits up, but couldn't muster the energy to do much else. Tom thought I was worried about him, making me feel guilty for my true longing. And I was scared. Since the sinking of the ship, it was assumed that sub was still prowling the waters off our coast. There was a rumor flying around town of a Jap plane flying over, but only one person had supposedly seen it, and he had a reputation for drinking a bit too much, so no one really believed it. Like me, people in town were fearful and pretty much stayed indoors. The Coast Guard with their canine unit continued to patrol the beaches, but nothing out of the ordinary was found. Life eventually went back to normal, or shall I say the new normal. I went back to work at Doc's office seeing the usual flow of patients, only now, Doc was giving me more responsibility, more doing than just watching.

One day he told me about the Red Cross training program and the need for volunteers. He offered to recommend me and pay any expenses I had, saying that I was well qualified and could help make a difference, despite the fact that I would be sorely missed here. At first, I rejected the idea out of hand. I couldn't leave Pa or Tom. Or could I?

That night over dinner I told Pa about it. He didn't say anything one way or the other, so I let it drop. He asked me how Tom was and I told him Doc had released him to return to work. His hand had healed fine and though it was still sore and he felt the pain in the finger that was no longer there—a phantom pain—he was okay.

I cleared the table and was starting to wash the dishes when Pa appeared at my side. "I want you to know, you don't have to stay here for me. I'll manage. I agree with Doc, you are needed elsewhere and can make a difference. I've seen it with my own eyes," he said as he squeezed my shoulder. "Do you want to go?"

I looked at him and didn't know what to say. I wasn't sure what I wanted to do and told him so.

"Well, you think about it and let me know what you decide," and with that he left the room.

I went back to washing dishes with my mind in a jumble. Should I go or should I stay? I'd never had to make such a decision before. I'd never really had to make any decision before that affected my life, my future. Which fabric to choose, what to order at Doyle's Fountain—that was the kind of decision I ever had to make. My life had just progressed, based on the events that happened around me. I did what I was told or whatever was asked of me. I'd been guided by my desire to be good, to be helpful, to be obedient, I was not the rebellious type, nor adventurous as some people my age were. Even my brother, who didn't think twice about leaving the safety and comfort of his home, went off to answer the call to arms. Could I do that? Could I leave the safety of my home, this town, Tom, Doc, the routine of my life to go to a city, to people I didn't know, to a new place to live, to days filled with unknown challenges and the endless stream of broken war-ravaged bodies that I would face?

How I wished Jane was here to give me her opinion. Jane Preston was my best friend. We'd met in kindergarten and grown up together; both our families had lived here since before we were born. We were a lot alike with similar personalities and demeanors, though Jane was decidedly more adventurous than I. Other kids called us "2J's", because we were pretty much inseparable. When we'd graduated, Jane went off to college, to Oregon State; she wanted to be a school teacher. We wrote to one another every week, but I truly missed her in my life, especially since the only other close friend I had, my mother, was gone too. I was surrounded by men who loved me, but there was no one to give me a female point of view about any hard choices I had to make, like now.

The dishes were done before I realized it. I didn't want to think about it anymore, closed the light, went to my bedroom and got ready for bed. I climbed under the covers and laid there, safe and warm, reading my favorite book, Pride and Prejudice, as far away from war as possible and fell asleep immersed in the world of Elizabeth and Mr. Darcy.

I woke the next morning and instantly knew what I would do. I needed to put aside my fears and anxiety and do my part, like Frank. And Jack. I would join the Red Cross program and help the men coming home to recover and heal. I told Pa as I was rushing out the door to go see Doc. He gave me his nod of approval and I was gone.

The next few days passed in a blur as arrangements were made for my departure. The only thing I really remember was telling Tom and him trying to talk me out of it. He said I wouldn't be safe, that we might get bombed. I told him that was unlikely. Then he tried to make me feel guilty about leaving him, that he wanted to get married. I amazed myself when I told him, steadfastly, that I needed to make this sacrifice as did he and that my mind was made up. I said I had to go, just like I knew he wouldn't hesitate to go if he were called, though I knew that wouldn't happen with his finger gone. We said our goodbyes and promised to write.

Soon, I was on the bus on my way to Portland, feeling sad for leaving my Pa and Doc, and Tom, the only place I had ever known, and also anxious about whatever was to come.

It had been a long bus ride and I was exhausted, but I was also exhilarated from my journey. Being on that bus by myself, then taking a taxicab from the station to this rooming house, seeing the busyness of a city, with all its many streets and buildings, cars, cabs, and streetcars, I felt a confidence I had never known, but wondered if I could keep from getting lost here. It was exciting but a little bit scary. Here I was in my new room, in a strange house, all by myself, no Pa to watch over me.

Mrs. Bell, the lady who ran the house seemed very nice, she made me feel very welcomed. It was after 8 o'clock when I arrived and the house was quiet. I hadn't eaten since noon, so she made me a sandwich and tea and we sat and chatted for a while so she could get to know me and tell me about how the house ran. She was a widow in her 60's and had owned this house for many years. It was close to the hospital, and with the large staff there, she never had trouble keeping the rooms filled. She told me I was lucky because the girl who had the room I was about to occupy had just gotten married to someone she met at the hospital and left to live with him. She told me there were eight rooms upstairs and two shared bathrooms, so for that reason, she only rented to young women, all of whom worked at the hospital. She was sure I would like it here, that I would make friends with the other girls, who I would meet at breakfast tomorrow, which was at 7 a.m.

She brought me upstairs, showed me the bathroom and then brought me to this lovely little room. It was small with one window, but then I didn't need much space and I wouldn't be spending much time in my room anyway. There was a bed, with a little table beside it, with a small hand-painted lamp, an upholstered chair, a small dresser and a closet. The bed cover, curtain and chair were all covered in pink chintz and had a very warm, homey feel. I liked the room, it was comfortable. I unpacked my suitcase and put my things away, took my toiletries and went for a bath.

Afterwards, I climbed into bed, feeling clean and sleepy from the warm water. My mind was running over the events of the day: my tearful goodbye to Pa before getting on the bus, riding for what seemed like an eternity over miles and miles of roads through places I'd never seen before, to the city and this house and Mrs. Bell. It was a bit of a blur, like a movie running at double speed. Yet, here I was in Portland, about to embark on a chapter in my life I was sure I would never forget. I suddenly felt very grown up, no longer a little girl and I was giddy with anticipation.

Out of the blue, I thought of Jack. Could he be here in Portland, at the hospital where I would be working? Oh, how I would love to see him again. He held a special place in my heart, which didn't make a whole lot of sense. I'd spent so little time with him, and knew so little about him and his life, but what I felt and what I knew, I really liked and I wanted to know more. He was so handsome and tall, I wanted to know what it would be like to be held by him, or kissed. I was swooning at the thought of being in his arms and realized I was acting like that silly girl I was trying not to be. With his image in my brain, I snuggled down into the warmth of the bed and promptly fell asleep.

*

I reported to the hospital in the morning and was given a tour, an indoctrination session and two uniforms to be worn whenever I was on duty. In no time at all, I got to know the facility, the procedures, where the supplies were and pretty much the routine of the ward. I was getting used to seeing the wounds, the blood, the pus, the amputated stumps and smelling the medicinal, disinfectant scent of a hospital. I was getting to know the other girls on the ward, who I worked so closely with, but all the while I was missing Jane. I wrote to her often, but it wasn't the same as talking face to face. Sometimes it would be more than a week before I got a response to a question I would ask.

In January, I received a letter from her. She was excited and had news to share—immediately I assumed she had met a boy and was engaged or something of the like. I was floored when I read that I had inspired her and she had enlisted in the WAVES, the newly created women's reserve of the Navy. She explained the acronym stood for Women Accepted for Volunteer Emergency Service, and that the Navy was desperate for men, thus was training women to do the U.S. land-based jobs, so the men could be released to the fighting arena. She was leaving in the morning for boot camp at Hunter College in New York City and would write me as soon as she knew her address.   She was excited and nervous at the same time, heading off to the big city. She didn't know what her job would be, but wanted to do her part for the war effort, as I was doing.

I was elated and proud—not just for her—but for myself, that I could actually inspire someone else. I immediately dashed off a response to her, sharing in her excitement, but then realized I would have to wait to mail it till I had her new address.

Pretty soon, whatever anxiety I felt about my new life faded away and I lived in a never-ending flow of men needing medicine, clean bandages, bedpans and sponge baths. It seemed like it would never end. These men had fought all over the world, in many places I'd never heard of. Each one was different, but yet all the same. All wounded, damaged both physically and mentally. Some were here for a matter of days and others much longer.

I'd managed to make some really good friends, girls like me, from other small towns. Some of them were staying at Mrs. Bell's. We'd laughed together and cried together, when it all became too much. We'd spent three Christmases together, and now three New Year's Eves, our President had been elected for a fourth term, and still the war cranked on. The good news was there had been no further attacks on our west coast after the sinking of the *Larry Doheny*, and my brother was alive and uninjured. All I knew of his whereabouts was that he was somewhere in the North Sea. His letters were short, never with details about what he was seeing or doing, just wanting to stay connected and to ask about what I was doing, so I wrote him often, and Pa, too. I missed him a lot, and wrote him long letters every week. I'd get a short note in return, letting me know he was okay, what he'd heard from my brother, what was going on in town. I occasionally got a letter from Doc with more somber news, updates on the medical issues of people I knew in town. He's the one who told me about a classmate of mine, Jimmy Dreyer, who had been killed recently in the Philippines, trying to recapture Corregidor from the Japanese. He was a sweet kid and too young to die. Though this war was being fought thousands of miles from here, it was still striking close to home.

Every now and then I received a letter from Jane and wondered if she ever received mine. She moved around quite a bit, so I couldn't be sure my letters would reach her, at least in a timely manner. After boot camp, she went to radio school in Ohio where she learned radio theory, procedures and Morse code. She said life in the military was hard: up early, long days and constant regimentation, everything on a schedule. The drilling and marching gave her blisters and she came to hate all the discipline, but she believed, or at least hoped, her efforts would help end the war sooner. She had been ordered to San Francisco, to Treasure Island, and was settling in there. Her work involved mostly communication with ships via Morse code but there was also teletype and voice transmissions.

She was getting to know her fellow radio operators—they worked closely in a small room—and liked being on a naval base and being so close to San Francisco, where there was always something going on, "unlike Port Orford where there was nothing going on." Her words stung and I suddenly felt sad. I could sense that she was slipping away from me and our hometown, which I longed to return to. Her life was filled with excitement and new experiences and new people and she loved it. And though mine was too, I knew I would willingly return home when the war was over, to my family, my job, to Tom. I continued to write to her to tell her about my life and experiences, to keep our friendship alive, but the time between our letters became further and further apart—I felt like we were two ships sailing in opposite directions. Then I got her letter saying she was transferring to Hawaii, to Pearl Harbor, and I had the unsettling sense I would never see her again.

As much as I missed her, Pa, Tom and home, I was very much enjoying my new-found independence. One of the friends I'd made here, Betty, was from Portland and knew the town very well. We went regularly to the movie houses where we kept up on the war from the newsreels, and saw films like *Destination Tokyo* which gave us some sense of what it was like to be on a ship embroiled in war, albeit glamorized, without the blood and maiming we were faced with on a daily basis. She knew where all the juke joints were and took us to dances at the enlisted men's club at Vancouver Barracks, just across the river in Washington or over to Corvallis to Camp Adair. I was even learning how to jitterbug, a new dance that was popular. I met a lot of young men there—enlistees—who were just passing through to an unknown place to risk their lives or their limbs. We all just wanted to have some fun and a few hours of normalcy, having a drink or dancing to the music of Glenn Miller or Duke Ellington, so as not to face the horrors and uncertainty of our lives. Like them, as long as I was laughing and having a good time, I didn't have to think about my brother who could be killed at any moment or Jimmy Dreyer, who would never laugh again. I met a young man from California who had big blue eyes who reminded me of Jack Long, made we wonder where he was. Perhaps he was back on an oil tanker or in some other godforsaken place getting shot at or maybe he was even dead.

At times, I had to contemplate how much longer it would go on; I felt like I was in a nightmare and couldn't wake up. It seemed like the tide was turning though. Each night in our rooms we'd listen to the updates on the war on the radio and knew that we'd recaptured the island of Guam from the Japanese and the allied invasion at Normandy had been successful, despite heavy losses, and led to Paris being liberated. The Soviet Army was making gains in the east as they drove on toward Germany. Soon both those forces would converge and hopefully squash the German army and force a surrender on that front. . . hopefully was the operative word.

But each day, we saw patients leave our wards and new patients fill their beds. There never seemed to be empty beds.

I realized I'd been sitting here awhile, as if in a trance, sipping my tea—that was now cold—my mind wandering, making me late for my shift.

Port Orford 1962

I'm sitting here looking out the window at a whale spouting as it crosses the bay, a common enough sight in this westernmost town in Oregon, where whales stop off for a meal on their migratory route from Alaska to Mexico. It seems one or two take up residence for a while here in this protected indent in the coastline, before they head south to breed and calve. It is such a peaceful sight, looking at all that calm, blue water. And then I look in the other directions—west, north and east—and all I see is destruction. We will have to fight our way back to being whole again.

It occurred to me that this storm is just another part of the history of this tough little town which got its start slightly more than a hundred years ago, with a bloody clash between white men and indigenous Indians, for which a historical marker points out Battle Rock, the site of that fight, to people passing through. And ever since, this town has been fighting for its survival. Through the Gold Boom of 1854, when gold was discovered on the beaches and hundreds of men came from all over to get rich, when the town boomed, hastily building hotels, shops and saloons. Two years later, it was all over. Most of the miners gave up, moved on, and Port Orford became a ghost town, with many shuttered buildings. Twelve years later, a forest fire nearly leveled the town, leaving two buildings and a barn. Were it not for logging, this town would have surely died then and there. But it did not, rebuilding, though not without setbacks. The success of the logging industry relied heavily on the dock, with transport by ship being the only way to get the wood to market. And how many times had tragedy struck there with newly-loaded ships foundering and the dock collapsing under the battering waves from the storms that rolled through here on a regular basis. Just last year, the dock collapsed with over a million board-feet on it; it took months to clear up the timber from the beaches and coves. Just as logging kept this town alive, it also brought death and hardship to many doors. So many men had been killed or lost limbs to logging accidents.

The same could be said for fishing. The bountiful sea brought many men to this little port who made a decent living hauling fish and crab. A cannery thrived here since the 40's, providing employment for many in the community. But now that is on the decline. The catches are smaller and regulations now limit when and how much fish one can take. And we've lost our fair share of men to the sea. . .the fishermen's memorial is testament to that.

But, thankfully, no one died in this last disaster, just a good part of the town. And, as in the past, buildings will be repaired or torn down and rebuilt stronger, the electric and phone lines will be restored, the trees will grow back just as they did after the fire of 1868. And Port Orford will go on through the booms and the busts, a tightly knit community of survivors. We have been called "the most independent people in the state of Oregon" and I think that is true. Based on our history and being so isolated, we rely on each other for survival.

Portland 1945

I was in the ward giving a sponge bath to a soldier who had lost a leg. It was August and ghastly hot, we'd been having a bit of a heat wave, so cool water helped to keep the men comfortable. We were chatting, me trying to cheer him up, when suddenly there was a great commotion. I could hear yelling and hoot-hollering out in the halls. Outside there were church bells ringing and car horns blasting. My first instinct was to drop to the floor, that we were under attack. Then, a nurse burst in through the door and yelled "It's over, it's over, the war is over," and just as quickly was gone. I looked at the young man in the bed and he looked at me with a big grin. He grabbed me and pulled me down for a big kiss. I was so surprised, I just let him do it. Moments later, he released the kiss and we were grinning like two fools, tears were streaming down his face. The excitement in the room was electric. Cheers of joy, tears, hugging—it was as if a huge weight had been lifted from us. For the first time in four years there was no threat, it was as if I heard a collective sigh, a release of the tension we'd all been holding for years. Betty came running over and we hugged and jumped for joy, both of us crying like little babies. At last, it was finally over. Our supervisor came into the room and told us nurses that yes, the Japanese had surrendered just as the Germans had a few months before. The fighting was over. She also said our work wasn't done here, that there would be many men coming now once all the prisoners were released and that she hoped we would stay until our help was no longer needed. And with that we went back to work, though our patients were decidedly happier and more animated than they were before the news.

That night, we nurses were allowed use of the phone for a quick call to our homes and I called Pa. It was so good to hear his voice. He told me Port Orford went crazy today with the news and there was lots of celebration. He asked me when I would be home and I told him there were so many patients here and yet to come, that we were still needed. But sensing the anticipation and a bit of loneliness in his voice, I promised I would be home before Christmas for sure, that I would come as soon as I could. I told him I had to go, there were a dozen girls behind me waiting to make a call. He told me he would tell Tom and we quickly said goodbye. The minute I hung up, I missed him and home in a way I hadn't in the three years since I'd gotten here.

The hospital remained full for the next couple of months, mostly with men coming from the prisoner of war camps. There were thousands of them and they were in horrible condition. They were suffering from malaria, beriberi and dysentery. Their bodies were emaciated and covered with all sorts of scars. These men had been starved, brutalized, beaten, bones broken, which healed poorly. They would suffer some of their injuries for the rest of their lives. But for the most part, their spirits were good. Some had been captive for over three years. They had survived their ordeal and couldn't wait to get home to their wives, girlfriends, families. We treated their sicknesses and their wounds and they got as much food as they wanted. We walked with them till they could walk on their own, we chatted with them and touched them gently to make them feel human again, and they responded quickly. When they left us, they were well physically and looked healthy, but their mental states were fragile. We hoped they would be able to withstand the bad news that surely some of them would meet back home, to assimilate back into a good family situation and to have the courage and patience to face the challenges of a society no longer at war.

By early December, the men had stopped coming and beds started to empty, as our patients recovered and went home. I told my supervisor I wanted to go home and she said she would make the arrangements for me. Before I left her office, she asked me if I'd given any thought to Nursing School, to going on to be certified. She told me that of all the nurses' aides she'd watched over the years, I was one of very few who seemed to have a calling for it, who remained undaunted and composed in the face of horrible, sickening scenes, treating every patient with compassion and respect and, most importantly, a smile. She said there was a school right here in Portland with a four-year program and she would be glad to recommend me. Overwhelmed by her praise, I thanked her and told her I would think about it.

Within a matter of days, I was on a bus heading south. Betty and a few of the other girls had a farewell celebration for me the night before. We'd all laughed and drank too much and cried when it was time to say goodbye. Now, I was tired and hunkered down in my seat for the long ride. My emotions were on a roller coaster. I was filled with memories—some good, some bad—of all the people I'd met who I, no doubt, would never see again. I was excited at the thought of Nursing School, of becoming a professional nurse. I would have to talk to Pa about it. I'd been away so long, another four years seemed selfish. Plus, I didn't know whether he could afford to pay tuition, it would be a lot.

The anticipation of what life would be like when I got home was unnerving. So much had changed, including me. I opened the Vogue magazine I'd bought in the bus station. With all the restrictions on cloth during the war, and being monotonously dressed in my nurses' uniform for so long, I wanted to see what the latest fashions were, what women were wearing now that Paris had been liberated and rationing was over. I wanted to think about something besides the war that had preoccupied my mind for these past years.

I was mindlessly flipping pages when I realized it was a different world, not just in fashion, but in every aspect of life. We'd gone through a world war, knowing more about geography than we'd ever learned in school. Being on the Pacific coast, our focus had been on the war with Japan, with fighting in the Pacific, and the possibility of being attacked on our home shores. All of the soldiers we'd treated were from that arena. But long before Pearl Harbor and the sinking of the *Larry Doheny*, there was a war going on in Europe, where the enemy was Adolf Hitler. He seemed rather maniacal to me by invading so many countries and enslaving its people. Most of what I knew about the war in Europe was from the newsreels we saw at the movies: The Battle of the Bulge, the Blitz, Normandy, the Battle of Stalingrad. I remember, about the same time I went to Portland, there was a rumor about the mass murder of European Jews. That rumor became fact when we saw photos and read about the concentration camps, mass graves and gas chambers, and estimates of some six million Jews being put to death, things too horrible to even contemplate.

We now had a new president who stepped in without a moment's hesitation when our beloved President Roosevelt died suddenly. Truman made the bold decision to drop atomic bombs on Japan to end the war. My God. Now we had a weapon that could destroy whole cities and hundreds of thousands of people in a matter of seconds.

Thousands of young men were coming home without a job and there were so many fewer jobs now that the war effort was over—no more planes, ships, tanks, jeeps, ammunition being made. Would we slide back into a depression? What would Frank do now that he was home? What would Pa do? He was a post-war casualty too, now that there was no longer a need for chromium, they closed down the mine where he'd worked. And what about me? Maybe Nursing School, or would I just become the keeper of my father's house? Would Tom still be interested in me, or, more importantly, would I still be interested in him? Our letters had been warm and friendly, but there was never any commitment on either of our parts. I had more questions than I had answers, and like so many thousands of men and women, I would just have to wait and see.

It was dark when I got off the bus and windy, as usual. That was one thing I hadn't missed. I was just about to go inside the station to call Pa to come get me when Tom rushed out the door. Before I could even ask how he knew I was there, be grabbed me in a big bear hug and kissed me madly—right there on the street—a long, wet tongue kiss that took me totally by surprise. I had never been kissed like that, so. . .so passionately. At long last, he released me from the kiss, held me at arm's length and we just looked at each other, taking in the vision before us, familiar but strange. Tom was older—more mature is probably more accurate—more handsome. He was manly, not a boy anymore, thicker, bulkier. He stared right back at me, which made we wonder how much I'd changed.

"You're prettier than ever," he said. I was sure I was blushing, but in the dark, he wouldn't see.

"And you are more handsome," I managed to get out, so astonished by the whole scene. "How did you know I would be here?" I asked.

"Your Dad told me you were coming in so I thought I would surprise you."

I laughed and said, "Well, you definitely did that."

"You must be hungry. Let's go over to CJ's and get a burger," he said as he started to lead me from the station.

"Oh, I don't know. Pa is probably waiting for me."

"No, I told him I would feed you before bringing you home in an hour," he said as he continued to push me along.

With that, I gave in; my stomach had been growling for quite a while. He grabbed my suitcase and my arm and we walked across the street to the grill. Inside, CJ came out from behind the bar to give me a hug and welcome me home. I'd known him my whole life and he made me feel like I really was home. He sat us in a booth and went off to get our food and a beer for Tom.

We spent the next hour getting to know one another again, catching up on our lives, things we'd done since my going away. We laughed and talked as we ate. I avoided talking about my work in the hospital. Tonight, I wanted to be light and gay and return to a sense of normalcy, to the time when I wasn't afraid and surrounded by carnage.

Port Orford 1946

Four months had passed; all my fears had been allayed and those questions I'd had were now answered. We'd had a wonderful Christmas, being together as a family for the first time in so long, and welcomed the new year with so much hope and promise.

Frank had moved to Portland where he started college, taking advantage of the GI Bill to pay for his tuition. He was studying engineering and seemed very happy with his life and his future. Pa had a new job at the sawmill which had reopened. There was a huge demand for lumber with the surge in house construction that was going on across the country for all the returning servicemen. There were quite a few mills in the area now and all were humming at capacity. Tom was working steady, too, supplying the logs to the mill. It was dangerous work, but he wanted to be outdoors and so far, was intact, minus the finger he'd lost.

I'd gone back to work with Doc, as his "nurse." I'd talked to Pa about nursing school and he said he would find a way to pay for it if I really wanted to go, but I was so happy being back home, I didn't relish the idea of leaving again—four years seemed so long. And, I was able to be a nurse here in this little rural community, though I knew it was the only place I would be able to do it without a certificate. The town was growing with all the work here and Doc was busier than ever, with two treatment rooms. He needed help and hired me as his assistant, there to prep the patients for him, taking blood pressure and temps, charting, cleaning any wounds. In this way, Doc could move between the two rooms, actually diagnosing and treating patients. He'd even had to hire a receptionist to take care of the phones and the books. The days flew by and I loved it. . .loved feeling useful and caring for people again. Plus, I knew I could always change my mind. If, in a year or two, I wanted to pursue the certificate, I was still young enough to do it.

Spring was in the air and the whole town seemed filled with vibrant energy, shrugging off the stormy, dark days of winter and war, and bursting with new life, new businesses, all thriving and blooming like the flowers on the trees. I was happy and couldn't remember a time when I'd been happier. I was content in this town and remembered Jane's comment about how dull it was. Perhaps dull to some, it was my home and I knew it always would be.

Port Orford 1951

Spring gave way to summer and this town was totally abuzz, had been for several months. We were about to celebrate our town's centennial, 100 years since Captain Tichenor claimed this land for his settlement in 1851. So much was planned for this day and, thankfully, it was a beautiful, sunny, windless day. Tom and I gathered up our little boys and headed into town for the celebration. Though Jimmy was only a baby, Tommy was two and old enough to enjoy many of the festivities. I pushed them in a carriage with a makeshift awning, trying to keep them both out of the sun.

We walked along Oregon Street which was blocked for traffic for the parade and greeted so many friends and acquaintances we hadn't seen in months. It seemed the whole town was on this street, many of them dressed in costumes like the early settlers of this town—women in long dresses and bonnets, men dressed as miners and farmers. I recognized many of the marchers as descendants of the early settlers of this town: from the Knapp, Tichenor, Lindberg, Masterson, and Hughes families. We blended in, stopping to view the old photos and sketches exhibited by the Historical Society showing the beginning of this town. I heard little Tommy laughing and clapping and saw several people dressed as clowns. He was ecstatic, so I took him closer. One of the clowns came over and handed him a lollipop, which he quickly grabbed. "Mama, want," he said, pointing at another clown blowing up balloons. The clown came over and offered him three different color balloons—red, white and blue—and asked Tommy which one he wanted. He reached out his hand to the red one and said, "bloon." I laughed and thanked the clown. Tommy couldn't have been happier, a lollipop in one hand and a balloon in the other, all the while Jimmy slept in the back of the carriage. I suggested to Tom we go down to Battle Rock, to watch the reenactment of the battle with the Indians. He said sure and we headed that way. About halfway there, we passed one of the open saloons, and Tom suggested I go on ahead. He was going to get a quick beer and meet me there.

Reluctantly, I agreed and went on down to the park, hoping to find a seat to watch the mock battle. I ran into our neighbors, Mary and her husband Ned, who graciously offered me his seat. They asked for Tom, who I said had made a stop and would be along shortly. Ned took Tommy for a short walk to stretch his legs and Mary held Jimmy, giving me a chance to dash to the ladies' room. By the time I got back, the ceremony was starting, with Tom nowhere to be seen. Tommy, now sitting on my lap, started bouncing and pointing. "Indins, Indins," as the men dressed as Indians came running toward Battle Rock brandishing their bows and knives. There were about 30 of them, though I knew the actual history recorded over 100 Indians versus nine white men. The man in the front, wearing a big headdress, presumably the Chief, yelled at the "white men" on top of the rock to leave. "Go from this place," he shouted. The men on top of the rock were firing cap guns and aiming rifles, pretending to shoot. A few of the "Indians" fell down. It was fairly amateurish but the children were loving it and they were learning our history. Soon the "Indians" started climbing the path up the rock, as the white men continued to fire. It seemed hopeless, as the "Indians" swarmed over the rock, closer and closer to their enemy, screaming something unintelligible. Just when it seemed they would be locked in hand-to-hand combat, there was a loud explosion and lots of smoke coming from the top of the rock where the white men and their smoking cannon stood. About half the "Indians" fell down and the rest, screamed in fright and

63

ran away. Little Tommy gasped and put his two little hands on his cheeks, he was just as surprised as anyone. The applause started as the fallen got to their feet and the fleeing returned to the base of the rock, all to take a bow. The crowd loved it, especially my son, who was clapping his hands gleefully, looked at me and said, "Again, Mama, again." It was such a wondrous moment. I looked around for Tom, and spotted him walking our way, and I was sad—he had missed the whole thing.

It was hard for me to truly enjoy the rest of the day's partying. Once again, I felt that emptiness that started on my wedding night and had never fully left me. Tom had chosen to be with his friends in a bar, rather than his wife and children. Now he wanted us to go on the boat ride across the bay, but Jimmy was fussing, so I begged off and stayed behind to feed him. Thankfully, Mary and Ned went with them, so I knew Tommy would be looked after, even if his father were negligent. When they returned, we walked back through town toward the park where food and refreshments were being served.

It was an extravaganza of food. I'd never seen anything like it. The local ranchers were all on hand, cooking and serving their products: grass fed beef steaks and hamburgers, pork sausages in different styles, Italian and German. The folks from Denmark, a tiny town just north of us, had a station where they served *frikadeller*, a type of Danish meatball, plus their version of sausage, with gherkins and rye bread, all foods from their culture. Langlois, the town further north, was represented by the namesake Market, serving their "world famous" hot dogs, which were locally made with a secret-recipe mustard and pickles on a bun; and the town's historical Cheese factory, which was serving wedges of their "famous" blue cheese. The potato farmers offered different varieties of potato salad, as well as baked and fried options. And for dessert, the dairy farm was churning several flavors of ice cream.

Not only was this a great spread of locally produced food, it was generously donated by these people who were direct descendants of the original settlers who came west right around the time Tichenor landed on our beach. They were celebrating their families' centennial as well as our town's. As I looked around at the many people dressed in old style clothes, I felt my own heritage here. My maternal great-grandparents, the McFarlins, had come west out of Massachusetts, bringing with them cranberry seedlings. They were instrumental in starting the thriving cranberry industry in Southern Oregon. Many people here today could tell stories of their ancestors starting ranches, farms, and businesses to make their living, passed down through generations to them, and still running today. I was proud to live in this town in Curry County, to be a part of what Frances Haelstrom, the poet, pegged, "the last frontier of the fading west."

Tom and I chose our food and then found a space at a table with some friends of his from work. One of the men I knew, but the other two were strangers. I said hi to Charlie and he introduced me to his wife, Ruth. Tom introduced me to the others who greeted me respectfully. Ruth motioned me to sit next to her, which I appreciated. We were on the end, so I could keep the carriage next to me to tend to my boys. Tom went and sat at the other end next to Rick. I started breaking up the hot dog I'd gotten for Tommy, which I knew he would eat. He was hungry and tried using two hands to get the food into his mouth; I had to take the plate away and only give him one little piece at a time. As I ate my own food, Ruth and I chatted. She was older than I and her two boys were off playing—there were so many activities for the kids here. When Tommy and I were finished eating, I decided to take him for a walk, so he might nap and asked Ruth to join me.

We walked around the park several times as both my boys napped, then stopped and sat on a bench as we watched her two boys with a large group of children kicking a ball around. Jimmy woke up crying, wanting to eat, so I discreetly put him to my breast, under cover of his blanket. It was a beautiful day, though a bit warm, and we sat for quite a while in the shade of a big old cedar tree, enjoying the breeze and each other's company and watching all the activity around us. Boys and girls of all ages were in the playground, and out in the fields playing softball, volleyball, kickball, shrieking with joy. It seemed a perfect day for young and old, here on the verge of the Pacific, oblivious to the fact our country was at war, on the other side of the ocean. I chose not to dwell on that thought, but rather the spirit of the day. We were celebrating one hundred years of courage and independence that drove the founders and our ancestors to this speck of land on the very edge of the continent, to adventure forth to the unknown, to barren land with only their hope for a future to sustain them. That independent spirit still thrived today, along with a sense of kinship and community we felt toward one another, like with Ruth, who I'd just met this day, but who shared with me the challenges and fears of being the wife of a logger.

As I put Jimmy back in the carriage, Tommy woke and wanted out, so I walked him over to the swings. Ruth offered to watch Jimmy for me, said she missed being around babies and I knew she understood it is always so much easier with just one to look after. Tommy loved the swing and giggled with each push. He couldn't seem to get enough of it until he spotted a little girl with an ice cream cone and pointing, said, "Mama, want."

After Tommy had his ice cream, which managed to drip all over his shirt, we went back to the table where we'd left the men. Tom called out to me when he saw us coming and it seemed he was slurring his words. They were all being loud and raucous. Ruth and I looked at each other, realizing at the same moment, they had been drinking. I sat next to Tom and took a sip from his cup. . .it felt like my mouth and throat were on fire. "What is that, it's so strong?" I blurted, feeling the heat in my stomach.

"It's mooshine. Good, huh?" he answered proudly, like I should be pleased he was drunk on someone's homemade alcohol.

The men were all looking at me, with the same silly expression as Tom. Trying to mask the fury inside me, I said as calmly and as sweetly as I could, "Yes, it's good, but the boys and I are tired and need to go home. We need you to walk us home."

"No, no, no, we're having too much fun," he slurred.

Before I could respond, Ruth came to my rescue, telling Charlie she wanted to go home as well—that it was getting late and we should all go home.

I rose and went to Ruth to give her a goodbye hug as I whispered "thank you" in her ear. Later, at home, with both Tom and Tommy passed out in bed from the excesses of the day, as I readied myself to join them, I tried hard to think of something other than my husband's drunkenness and thought of the day's celebration and how momentous it had been. When so many little towns in this state had been abandoned and just ceased to exist—become ghost towns—Port Orford was alive and thriving after one hundred years. With thoughts of both pride and joy, I drifted off to sleep.

Seeing the fireworks on the television, my mind went back to this past July, when we celebrated the centennial of our state. With many of the same events as our town centennial, celebrating 100 years of statehood was even more spectacular, including our first-ever fireworks display. Never having seen fireworks before, it was a memory I would not soon forget. I remembered sitting on Battle Rock beach with Tom and our four kids, as we watched in amazement the kaleidoscope in the sky—the bursts of color and changing formations—listening to the booms and the shrieks of the little ones, though I was even more awestruck than they. What fun it was.

Now, here on the news there were fireworks to celebrate a new state, Hawaii, which they just reported was the 50th state to become part the United States. I thought of Jane who was still there. When she was first stationed there, she'd met Kala, a local Hawaiian fisherman, who delivered fish to the base. She said she fell in love with him the first time she saw him and when he spoke, in his soft and calm voice, she was hooked. They married when she was discharged from the WAVES and soon had two children. This past Christmas I'd received a card from her with a picture of her family. How different from us they looked in their floral shirts and dresses, and her with long, flowing hair and a flower behind her ear, a young boy and girl by her sides and being held by a handsome, dark-skinned man. A beautiful, happy family, sitting under a palm tree in front of the ocean with a mountain in the distance. What an exotic place it must be, and then I thought of the irony, that this warm place followed a cold place, Alaska, in joining the U.S. in this same year, 1959. Two states in one year, when there hadn't been a new state in over 40 years. I turned off the television and laughed to myself, thinking about these strangely exotic places, and how I had never been out of the state of Oregon, other than my little jaunts into Washington during the war.

I was halfway down the hall, when I felt like I'd been punched in the stomach, with all the air forced out of me. I couldn't believe what I had just overheard. I was on my way into the den where Tom and his long-time friend Johnny were polishing off a 12-pack, getting louder and more raucous by the minute. I was going to try to dissuade them from further drinking or bring them some food to sop up the alcohol, when I heard Johnny say, "Quit the bullshit, Tom. You and I both know you purposefully put your finger under that chain. You wanted to lose it so you wouldn't have to serve. It's cool. I mean I was pretty happy when they rejected me cause of my feet, but I wouldn't have chopped off a finger or toe to get out of it. So, don't try to bullshit me that you were sorry you didn't go."

"I am sorry. I didn't get to see the world or get the respect or admiration veterans get; I see the way my wife looks at anyone in a uniform. And I don't get the benefits they got. Like my brother-in-law. He's a hotshot engineer up in Portland. Got to go to college for free. Now he goes to the country club and plays golf," Tom said sarcastically as he opened another beer. "What'd I get. Work my ass off for the man, risking my life every day for a measly little paycheck."

I couldn't believe what I was hearing. I slumped down on the floor feeling totally numb. This man I'd lived with all these years, trusted and mostly respected—he did drink too much—was a liar and a fraud. When he'd lost that finger, he went on and on about how sorry he was that he couldn't serve his country. Tears filled my eyes and I realized what a con he was, a weak, pitiful excuse for a man. I sat there in disbelief listening to them laugh and belch. Eventually, I pulled myself up and went to bed, though I really wanted to walk out the door and run far away.

I tossed and turned for hours and at some point, fell asleep from sheer exhaustion. How was I supposed to un-hear what I heard? Could I forget it and just carry on for the sake of my kids? They loved him. He spent time with them, when he wasn't working or drinking, which seemed to be consuming more and more of his time. He had become a drunk.

He'd never hit them or me. He yelled a lot and was pretty rough in bed, but then he'd never been the lover I had dreamed of. Always taking what he wanted, even if I didn't want to. That's why I'd had a baby every year, until I got sterilized. I'd always wished he'd been a little gentler, a little smoother but he was Tom, a tough logger. He'd been a good provider and I don't think he'd ever cheated on me. But he'd done something unforgiveable, cowardly. I'd seen first-hand the thousands of men who'd answered the call of duty despite the risks and their fears. And here I was married to a coward. How could I get beyond that?

*

Ever since that night I had lived a lie, just as Tom had for all these years. I'd put up the front of being the happy housewife for my kids. I wanted them to have the life that Tom provided: a nice house, plenty of food, whatever shoes and clothes they needed. Plus, they needed a father, sorry excuse though he was. In many ways, he was good to them, and he spent time with them, when he wasn't drunk. But I didn't love him or respect him—not anymore. I'd put my sense of honor aside for the sake of my kids. I didn't want them to suffer as I and, surely, Tom was. That was probably why he drank so much, he couldn't live with what he'd done. I never let on in front of the kids. I wanted them to think their dad was a good, decent man. I played my part well. I did whatever I needed to do to create a harmonious, happy home for them. I covered up my loathing for him, with a happy-wife persona to keep peace in our home. At least until they were grown. Tommy was ten. In eight years, he'd be out of school. Maybe join the military and learn a skill that he could parlay into a good job, a safe job that would save him from logging or fishing and putting his life on the line every day. Then Jimmy would follow the next year, then Mary. In 10 years, she would be ready for college to become a teacher or maybe go to nursing school, to pursue nursing in a way I never got to. I would insist with Tom that we start a college fund for them, so they would have chances we didn't have as children.

And then there was Amy, she was only six. It would be 12 years before she would graduate and then another 4 years of college. Sixteen years. . .I might have to put up this charade for sixteen years before I could leave this dishonorable man. He just disgusted me. When I thought about all the thousands of sailors and soldiers I'd met and the thousands more I never got to meet, who went bravely, without question, to serve their country. Men like my Pa, who fought in WWI and who lived his whole life with honesty, integrity and pride in his country, who always did whatever he had to do for his family, regardless of whether it made him happy or not.

I could do it. I would do it. For my kids. They were everything to me. They were the good that came out of my marriage to Tom—Tommy, Jimmy, Mary and Amy, my baby. I remembered her birth, like it was yesterday; how precious and special she was to me, knowing she would be my last. I remember waking up to the nurse calling my name. She was bringing me my newborn baby girl. Amy was going to be her name. She was a beautiful little girl and I savored every precious moment with her knowing there would be no more. I had told Doc to sterilize me after this birth—my fifth in five years. After my last child was born dead and I found myself pregnant again a few months later, I knew it had to stop. After each birth, Tom would give me a couple of months to recover and then would pile on me night after night. He never seemed to be too sick or too tired, though sometimes he was too drunk. It was like he couldn't sleep unless he screwed me. I can't say "made love to me" because most of the time I was a non-participant, an unwilling vessel, a dutiful wife. I wondered if he would be happy or sad that there would be no more children. I think my being pregnant was like a badge for him, to show the world that he was virile, a "real" man.

Little Amy started to fuss, her mouth was moving a mile a minute. She was hungry and wanted to suck. I lowered my gown and put her to my breast. She knew instantly what to do, such a smart girl. I thanked God for bringing her to me—a healthy, perfect baby—and feeling blessed to be holding this little bundle of joy, just as I'd done with my other three. My children were my life and I had Tom to thank for that. They gave me such joy, so much pleasure. *He* wasn't perfect, but they were.

Portland 1942

Each morning when I arrived at the ward, there would be a list of men who would be leaving that day. They were the first priority. For those who were going home, I needed to get them washed, shaved and dressed in a new uniform, so they would look nice for the family or friends they were returning to. Others were being transferred to different facilities for further care or for rehabilitation. My heart broke for these men. They were missing something they would have to learn to live without—a hand, an arm, a foot, a leg, sometimes more than one. We had to groom them and change their bandages for their journey. Saying goodbye to them was hard to do. . .you couldn't help but feel personally attached to them.

The last man on the list was Sam Gunderson, from Crescent City, California. He'd been here about two weeks and I was the only nurse he would let touch him. He'd lost an arm to a mortar shell and was burned a good deal about his chest. Every day I would clean and re-bandage his wounds. Nursing wounds like his is such an intimate act that forges a closeness, a bond almost like a lover. I had this feeling for so many of these men. I remembered the first man I'd ever treated this way— Jack Long. Oh, how many times I had thought of him. Every man I treated with burns made me think of him and wonder where he was, alive or dead. He's the one I didn't get to say goodbye to, not like these men. Not like Sam. Our banter this morning was light and gay to mask the sadness of his leaving. Just as I finished taping the last bandage, some men came in with a gurney for him. He was being transferred to a rehab center in California. I held his hand and wished him well, told him to have courage, that he would learn to live without his arm. He squeezed my hand so hard I felt confident that he would do just that. I was holding back my tears; I didn't want him to see me cry. I lightly kissed him on the cheek, said goodbye and stepped out of the way. He was special to me, because we were both from coastal towns, and thus had shared experiences, memories of childhood that were so similar. I would miss talking to him. They transferred him quickly and soon were wheeling him away. He turned his head back to look at me and threw me a kiss, "Bye, Jenny," and he was gone out the door.

I stood there feeling that emptiness I'd felt so many times before, whenever someone left I'd gotten to know and like. I was thinking about Sam when Betty came up to me, handed me clean sheets and said, "We need to get these beds remade. We've got new ones coming in." I snapped out of my trance and got to work. There were more men coming in. Always more men.

The day started out like any other with the usual crowd, plus a few tourists passing through. You would see them once or twice, and then never again. I was at the register cashing a couple out when in walked a stream of people. Two, four, eight, twelve, I lost count but they still filed in. By the time I got to them, to seat them, there were 24 of them. Holy cow, this was going to be not fun. They looked like a bunch of bird watchers with the binoculars and cameras around their necks. I asked if they were together. The gentleman in the front said, "Yes, we are part of a group but we don't expect you to seat us together." He laughed as he said that last part. I looked around. I didn't have enough seats.

"I can seat most of you now, but some of you will have to wait a few minutes." All the while I was wondering how Verna and I, and CJ for that matter, were going to handle all these people at once. They were fine with that, said they weren't in a hurry, so I started seating them. CJ saw what was happening and got the dishwasher cleaned up to help us out. He could bring them water and coffee if they wanted it and to quickly bus tables for anyone who was ready to leave. I seated all but four of them and then Verna and I started taking orders, one table at a time to pace the cooking for CJ.

"Good morning," I said as calmly as I could muster. "How are you all this fine day?"

"Fine, fine. Just hungry," one said.

"Okay then, what would you like?" I focused on the one lady at the table, took her order and continued on from there.

At last, we got them all seated and fed without anyone losing their patience. They were a nice group, jovial even. I asked what their group was. The same gentleman who had taken the lead earlier told me they were the POMA, The Port Orford Meteorite Association. Seeing my blank expression, he went on to explain that they were searching for a "national treasure," a 10-ton hunk of rare metal they dubbed, "The Rock."

"I was born in this town and grew up hearing about this great rock, but we all know that's just a myth," I said trying to keep a straight face.

"Oh, it's real" he retorted, very sternly. "It was discovered and documented a hundred years ago, a sample of it sits in the Smithsonian in Washington, D.C."

"Well, if it was documented, why do you think it's never been found?" I asked, seriously.

"Well, the man who discovered it was on a mapping expedition for the Congress at the time and died before he could get back here to retrieve it. So, we just go by the notes he kept in his journal, looking for the geography as he described it."

"But for years, there have been reports of people searching for it and never finding a trace. How long have you been looking for it?" I asked curiously.

"We've been coming here every spring and fall for the last several years. We would love to find it for the sake of science, but most of us do it for the fun and the adventure."

"Well, I wish you good luck and we'll hope to see you in the fall," I said as I moved toward the register. They all paid their checks and filed out just as they had filed in. I laughed to myself when the last one left, thinking about this big rock. Port

Orford's only claim to fame, other than Battle Rock, and it was either a myth or a hoax.   Or, perhaps it was still sitting there in a much-changed landscape just waiting to be found.

Port Orford 1945

After a while, I found life settled into a routine. The town had its own rhythm and being so small, we were all connected in some way. When good things happened, we rejoiced together, and when tragedy struck, we all mourned. We celebrated births and deaths as one big family. That first year after the war was cause for celebrations of holidays on a much larger scale. That Christmas, aside from any private family rituals, what started out as a few folks getting together for Christmas dinner, turned out to be practically the whole town having that meal at the Grange. Each family cooked its traditional dishes and brought them over. The men set up the tables and folding chairs that were kept there for meetings, annual dinner dances and new year's celebrations. The long food table was soon laden with turkeys, hams, gooses, bowls filled with mashed potatoes, sweet potatoes and every kind of vegetable you can imagine, plus corn bread, biscuits and rolls. Some men started carving and then folks just helped themselves. I didn't have much of a cooking repertoire, but Pa always said my green bean casserole was the best, so I made that and a batch of cookies for the dessert table. I had never seen so much food in one place at one time. Hour after hour people kept drifting in, folks giving up their seats as they finished eating so the newcomers could sit. There was pop to drink—a real treat—and beer, of course, all donated by CJ.

A few men had brought their musical instruments so we had music throughout the day—guitars, fiddles, banjoes, even a washboard. We all joined in as the women from the different church choirs sang Christmas carols and other hymns. Everyone had a great time, young and old, well-off and poor, friend and foe, though on that day we were all friends. The war was over, almost everyone had come back; we shirked off our fear because there was no longer any threat of being attacked. The Depression was over too. Men had jobs and were making good wages, families were prospering. People had hope again and maybe a little too much bravura. Now that we had "the bomb," some people said we were unbeatable, that we would never be attacked again.

That day brought out the best in everyone. There was laughing and singing, lots of hugging and sharing. I think it will be one of the best memories I have of this town, when we were all one.

Tom and I had eaten together and when we were finished, he asked me to go for a walk with him, which I was more than glad to do. The room was hot and stuffy and I was feeling quite full. We put on our coats and went out. It was a clear and sunny day but the wind was out of the north and cold. He held my hand and we walked along the river toward the ocean, away from the Grange. When we were out of sight, he pulled me into his arms and to my great surprise, kissed me hard, with unbridled passion. I succumbed to his embrace and my own desire and kissed him back. His mouth was warm and savory and as he pulled me in closer, I could feel his hardness pressing against me. I was lost in my own lust but felt him pulling me down. Realizing we were getting a little too carried away, I wiggled free and held him at arm's length, both of us panting like dogs.

"I'm sorry," he said, trying to catch his breath. "I just love you so much."

"You don't have to say sorry. I enjoyed the kiss, too," I responded as I tried to regain my composure.

"I think it's time we got married," he blurted out.

That word sent my mind running in a dozen directions. Married. . .I wasn't ready for that. I'd only been home a few weeks and yes, we'd seen each other almost every day and I liked him a lot, but I just wasn't in the same place as he. "Oh, Tom, we have lots of time for that," I managed to say.

He pressed on. "I know we have time, but I know you're the one I want to spend the rest of my life with."

I didn't want to blurt out a rejection, to hurt his feelings, so I told him the truth, in as nice a voice that I could muster. "Look, Tom. I'm not ready to say yes now. I just got back and need time to settle into this new life. I'm enjoying my work and I don't want to give that up yet."

"You don't have to give it up. Not right away. Not until a baby comes along," he said still trying to convince me.

A baby. Marriage and a baby. This really was too much for me to accept right now. I wanted to work, to hold onto some of the independence I'd discovered. I needed to know Tom a lot better. . .I needed to know myself a lot better, before I could say yes. "Tom. You are the only man in my life, but I need time. I just can't say yes right now. Please, if you love me as you say you do, you'll give me time to sort out my feelings, to grow into marriage. Please. We're young and have plenty of time."

He looked at me, took a deep breath and said, "Alright, we'll take our time." He smiled and reached for my hand. I squeezed his tightly, smiled back at him and we started our walk back.

The reveling went on for hours, until well after dark. The musicians played on and couples danced. It was a celebration of life and peace we did not want to end. I helped other women pack up whatever food was left and give it to those just getting by, mostly widows.   People started to leave, the ones with children, wanting to get them to bed. Then just as the day had unfolded, it retreated, as the lights went out, the door was locked and the last car left the lot. We all went back to our homes and our lives, thinking we were safe and free, that war with all its sacrifices was over for good and there would be everlasting peace on earth.

Port Orford 1946

Tom must have suggested we get married a half-dozen times. We were becoming more and more attracted to one another. We were both feeling desire and it was growing stronger each time we were together. The last time we were alone in his truck, I almost gave into him. My body felt electrified. My breasts were tingling and I felt on fire between my legs. I was wet with lust for him, his kisses driving me crazy, making me ravenously hungry for him. He lay on top of me, rubbing himself on me as we both moaned with pleasure. He was going faster and faster until we both exploded in orgasm and fell limp. We lay there silently for some time, covered in sweat, breathing heavily. We sat up and smiled at each other, not knowing quite what to say.

"You okay?" he asked.

"Yes, I'm fine," I managed to say but was thinking of other words that were more descriptive of how I felt: happy, satisfied, relaxed. Then realizing my panties were soaked, I said, "I think I need to go home now."

He nodded and said "sure" and drove me home.

It was late when I got home and Pa was asleep. I washed and put on my nightie and climbed into bed. I lay there remembering the night and what I had felt and asked myself what I was waiting for with Tom. Surely, I loved him. . .I certainly desired him. Why not get married and make love for real, get to know what it would feel like to have him inside me. Yes. It was time. Tomorrow I would tell him and we would make plans for our wedding. I fell asleep feeling resolved and happier than I ever remember feeling.

I woke the next morning feeling alert and refreshed, anxious to tell Pa and Tom my decision. It was Sunday and Pa was at the table drinking tea, which I don't ever remember seeing him drink—he was a coffee drinker.

I kissed him good morning and remarked, "You're drinking tea. You feeling okay?"

"Oh, I slept kind of poorly and I thought maybe all that coffee might be keeping me awake."

I looked at him and realized he was very pale and looking rather haggard. His face also looked thinner. I hadn't seen much of Pa the last few weeks, both of us had been busy working and I'd been out a lot with Tom.

"Other than last night, are you feeling okay? You look a little pale," I commented.

"Oh, I'm fine. I'll rest up today and be good as new tomorrow."

"Okay, let me fix you some breakfast. What'll it be, eggs or pancakes?"

"Nothing for me. I think I'm going to lay down and see if I can't sleep a bit," he said as he got up to leave.

"Okay, I'll fix you something when you get up."

He kissed me on the forehead and retreated to his room, where he stayed most of the day. I busied myself with chores and thoughts of my wedding and Tom and the day passed quietly by. At supper time, all he wanted was some soup. When he finished it, he said he wanted to go back to sleep, so I kissed him goodnight and let him go.

The next day, Pa didn't go to work, saying he didn't feel up to it. He looked worse than he did yesterday and I noticed he really had gotten thinner; his clothes were hanging on him. I convinced him to come with me to see Doc.

They were in the examination room for quite some time when Doc called me in. Pa was fully dressed and sitting on the exam table. Doc told me to sit in the chair and I started to get a bad feeling, like he was about to tell me bad news, which he did. Pa's heart was bad—it was enlarged. He would need to take time off from work and rest and take some medicine every day to try to stabilize his heart.

Doc was still talking but I wasn't listening. I was thinking that my Pa was going to die and I would have to live without him, just like Mama. Since she died, he and I were dependent on one another. We'd grown very close, especially since Frank left home. I loved Pa with all my heart and I just couldn't imagine life without him. My mind was rambling all over the place and I was filled with such sadness. I felt someone touch my arm and I heard my name. It was Doc, "Jenny, are you with me?" I heard him say. "Yes, yes," I blurted, "What can I do to help Pa get better?" I asked as I rose to stand by him to hold his hand.

"Just make sure he gets lots of rest. Follow the diet I'm going to give you and make sure he takes these pills, one every 12 hours."

"Of course," I said trying to smile at Pa, who looked so forlorn. I didn't want him to know how upset and afraid I was. Doc told me to take the rest of the day off and take Pa home, to get him to lie down and have something light to eat. And to give him another pill before bedtime tonight.

We went home and I ministered to Pa. I read through the diet to learn what he should and should not eat. While he rested, I went to the market to buy some of the things on this new diet. Pa became my only thought. He was all that mattered to me now. I would have to let Frank know. And Tom. Any thoughts of a wedding and marriage were driven from my mind. After a supper of hearty vegetable soup that I made for him, we sat in the parlor, listening and laughing at *The Bickersons* on the radio, enjoying each other's company, both of us pretending not to be afraid.

Port Orford 1950

The radio was playing "Happy Days Are Here Again" as I prepared our dinner, which seemed so incongruous. It was hard to remember the peace and optimism I felt just five years ago. Not just me, the whole country and much of the world had let out a sigh of relief, a release of so much pent up anxiety now that the war was over. We had won. We thought life could go back to normal, to life as we knew it before the war, with thoughts of everlasting peace. But of course, that could not happen; the world was changed forever. Almost immediately, that anxiety returned when our ally, the Soviet Union, became our enemy. They started grabbing up land in all directions, creating what we came to know as the "Iron Curtain," the veil of communism that took away people's freedom. And now we were at war again, trying to save the little country of South Korea from the Soviet-backed Chinese invasion from the north. The China that had allied with us to defeat the Japanese, was also now our enemy. How many men would be sacrificed this time? Thank God, my children were just babies. But what kind of world had I brought children into? A world where no one was safe. Now that the Soviets had the atomic bomb, we were no longer untouchable, immune from attack. A bomb could drop on us at any time. Even if we had a bomb shelter, like many of our neighbors were building, you couldn't live in one of those forever.

I tried to stay positive and hopeful that our government, our leaders, would protect us, tried to think about things closer to home. We were thriving here in Port Orford. Tom was working steady and making good pay. There were now 12 sawmills and they just kept devouring the trees as fast as they could be cut down. Houses were going up all over the country as GI's got married and started families—there was an insatiable appetite for wood. We had married two years ago, after Pa died. Pa had lasted about two years, growing weaker and feebler with each passing week. But he and I grew closer, spending practically every minute together, when I wasn't working. We watched television, a new invention that was catching on, that Frank had bought for him. He loved Milton Berle and *The Ed Sullivan Show*, with acts from all over the world. I was so thankful to have had that time with him, but I miss him every day, still.

Our wedding was a lovely ceremony up at the Castaway Lodge, overlooking the harbor. It had been a beautiful day and a beautiful setting, a small, intimate wedding with few attendees. We were married on the front lawn, then had dinner at the Lodge with our guests: Tom's mother, his best friend, Johnny, my brother Frank and his wife, Jane's parents who'd sort of adopted me, and, of course, Doc. I think that was the first time I drank champagne. It tickled my nose and made me giddy.

We had our wedding night there as well, in the bridal suite. It was a lovely room but I hardly noticed. We were both tipsy from the champagne and filled with lust, bottled up for years. Once the door closed, we were ravaging each other. Kissing, groping, stripping off clothes until we fell on the bed and I felt Tom jam his hard penis inside me. I felt pain and something popped, but we didn't stop. He was moving in and out of me quickly and deeply and then he made this growling sound and stopped. I wanted him to keep going, I was still so aroused. I wanted him to keep moving in me so that I could feel the same ecstasy I knew he had felt. I told him so and he said he couldn't, that he was finished. He said to be patient that I would have many more chances and promptly fell asleep.

Two more times that night he woke me up, fondled me, then climbed on top where he took his pleasure telling me how happy he was that we were married, that we could do it whenever we wanted. He kissed me and I tried hard to feel close to him, but quite the opposite was true. I felt alone and abandoned, like I was sleeping with a stranger. I cajoled myself with the idea it was the champagne and the newness of our marriage and that soon we would develop a close, intimate partnership, filled with love and mutual respect.

Within a few weeks, I knew that was not to be. Tom's "lovemaking" remained constant, almost every night, but was a one-sided affair. It was like he owned me. I had never felt that way in my whole life. I also knew that I was pregnant. I hadn't bled and my body felt different, not in any way I could articulate. I just felt different. I hoped I was. I hoped there would be someone else to share my life with. Someone who would love me unconditionally, who I could dote on and laugh with, someone to rescue me from my isolated existence. Yes, I had Tom, we were married, but that seemed to be just a legality. And yes, he was a good provider, he'd bought us a house right away and brought home plenty of money. And yes, we had fun together, but we were not connected on any deep, emotional level—there was a void. Like our hearts were beating together, but not entwined, not the oneness of our souls I wanted. I hoped a child would bring us closer, to an intimacy that only life created together could bring. But that turned out not to be the case. We shared that fleeting intimacy for a few minutes when Tom first visited me in the hospital, to see his son, but then we were back to our same detached relationship.

I turned the radio off and finished getting dinner ready, when I heard the door open and close. I went excitedly to greet Tom, and to tell him I was pregnant again.

At last I had a baby girl and was overjoyed. Not that I was disappointed when my first two were boys, but I was thrilled to have a daughter that I could share a special connection with, as I had with my mother. Oh, how I missed her. She wasn't there for all those special moments in my life. . .my graduation, my wedding, the birth of my children that would have been her grandchildren. Now I could shower all my attention on this little girl, as my mother had done with me: dressing her in pretty clothes, teaching her deportment, making cookies and pies, shopping for fabric and making dresses together, being her companion and her friend, taking her to the toy store to let her choose a new piece of furniture for her doll house, or a new storybook to read together. I cherished those memories of my mother. As a young girl, she was the most important person in my life and I loved spending time with her. She was fun and funny. Whereas Pa was quiet and serious, she was the light of the house, always finding the good, always with a funny tale to tell of her own childhood. And she was so pretty. Fair with golden hair and twinkling green eyes, which she'd passed on to me. But then I remembered how all that changed. . .she got sick. I was 15 and, unwittingly, became an adult very quickly.

That next year was one I would like to forget: her going off to the hospital and coming home looking older and weak, the twinkle in her eyes gone; caring for her as she lay in her bed wasting away, growing thinner, weaker, in more and more pain; washing her, combing her hair, changing her clothes and bedding. I was willing to do anything for this woman I loved so much, including, reluctantly, being the lady of the household:

cooking, cleaning, shopping. I missed a lot of school, but the teachers understood and allowed me to do the assignments at home. I told them that as soon as my mom was better I would be back at school. I was naïve and didn't understand what was happening to my mother. I didn't have the faintest idea about cancer. I'd never heard of it before and never knew of anyone who'd had it.

Not long before she died, my mom made me sit and listen to her. She gave me a bit of an anatomy lesson and told me she had cervical cancer. She told me about how she first knew something was wrong, that she felt pain in her pelvis and her bleeding had grown very heavy. She went to the hospital, where she was treated with radium tube insertions and then x-rays. It all made her feel dreadful, sapping her strength and making her feel nauseas. She had no appetite, which I could well attest to—getting a few sips of soup or honeyed tea in her was the best I could hope for. And then she told me she would not get well, that the cancer was eating away inside her. I was crying hysterically but she made me stop. She made me promise that I would be strong for her—she needed me to do that for her and for my brother and father—and that I would look after them, but to have my own life, too. They could learn to take care of themselves, but she had high hopes for me, to be more than a housewife, as she had been. She also made me give my word that I would be more vigilant about my own health, that in time there would be a test for what she had, a way to detect it earlier, that Doc had told her about the research. She literally made me swear.

Whenever I was alone, I would cry; my heart felt like it was being torn apart. I couldn't bear the thought of losing my mother. She not only gave me life and nurtured me, she was my best friend, my constant companion, my whole world. It was all so hard to believe. She was so young, just 40 and she was withering before my eyes. At some point, I realized I was just being selfish, that this was not about me. It was my mother who was dying, giving up life. She seemed resigned to her death, but I wondered if she had any regrets. Or if there were things she hoped to accomplish in this life that she hadn't gotten to yet. I was filled with sorrow, but I knew that I had to be strong for her, I couldn't let her see me cry. I didn't want her to see how truly sad and broken I was.

The next month she was mostly out of it. Doc came every morning to check on her and give her a shot of morphine. Then he taught me to do it, so I could give her a shot whenever she needed it, which was more and more with each passing day. One night she asked me to get my brother and father. We sat with her, me holding one hand and my father the other. She told us she loved each of us in a special way but that it was time to say goodbye. It was hard, so very hard. My brother kissed her and ran from the room, unable to let anyone see him cry. My father and I took our turn. And then she closed her eyes, took a few breaths and was still. I saw the stress drain from her body and felt her hand lose its grip. She was gone, along with all her pain and suffering. At last, she was free from the grip of the cancer and at peace.

Pa dried his tears and left the room to call Doc. I stayed and continued to hold her lifeless hand, not quite ready to let go. I tried to remember her laugh and all the wonderful, fun times I had with my beautiful mother, and how loved she always made me feel. I couldn't remember one time my mother ever yelled at me or my brother, she had such a wonderful manner. If we did something wrong, she would ask us why we did it and if we thought it was right or wrong. Of course, when she confronted us like that we always knew it was wrong. And we learned—because we wanted to please her— how to be the best we could be. I only hoped one day I would be as exceptional a mother as she and to be blessed with a daughter to love in the same way. I wanted to make my mother proud of me, to be her legacy, a respectful and respectable human being.

So here I was, missing her still, but holding a beautiful little baby with dark hair and long eyelashes and the cutest little pink mouth. I kissed her and hugged her close and told her I loved her, and because I knew her grandmother would love her just as much, her name would be Mary, after my mother, who continued to be the light of my life. I was beaming at her, feeling her fill my heart and looking forward to creating fun times and wonderful memories for her, just like my mother had for me.

Port Orford 1959

My mother had high hopes for me, wanting me to be more than a housewife, but that is exactly what I had become, and now that seemed all the more burdensome. I dropped the kids off at school, mindful of their fragile states, giving each one a reassuring hug. I continued to restrain my own emotions, as I waved them off and got back in the car. I didn't go home. I kept driving. I wanted to run away, to escape my fears, the doubts, the sea of uncertainty I now found myself in. I drove north on the 101, with no destination in mind, until I saw the sign for Cape Blanco and made a quick left turn. I needed the beach.

Out near the lighthouse, I parked my car and took the trail down the hillside. On the beach, I started walking and before I knew it, I was running, running hard like I was being chased. Chased by some ominous creature. And I was. Chased by my grief that soon overtook me, I burst into tears and fell to my knees. Tom was dead, killed violently three days ago by a runaway log after a cable snapped. My children were now fatherless and devastated by the loss—getting them to school today took all my powers of persuasion and pretense. Alone at last, this was the first time I'd allowed myself to cry, to feel the sorrow that filled me, and let the deep well of tears gush forth. I was sobbing, my body convulsing, wracked with trembling, more for them than for me. My love for Tom had died many years ago, and there was so much about him I would not miss at all. I was sad that his life had ended so violently—I prayed he never saw it coming—and that his short life was filled with so much regret, turning him to alcohol to escape. I was crying because he was the breadwinner, the total support for our family. Now we were. . . adrift. I was crying for myself. For the first time in my life, I felt truly alone.

After some time, the well dried up and my tears stopped and I sat there on the beach, looking aimlessly out to sea, realizing it was all up to me. I had to become the head of the household. But how? I wished now I had gone to nursing school. Since Doc had retired and left town, and without a certificate, nursing was not an option. I wasn't qualified to teach school, nor did I have the skills to become a secretary, not that there were any of those jobs in this town anyway. I thought of all the widows in this town and the directions they took to keep a roof over their heads and food on the table for their kids. I could become a merchant, but there wasn't any kind of business I could think of this town needed. And I didn't have any special talent or skill that people would pay me for. Then I thought of Frank. If all else failed, I could always move to Portland, where I knew my brother would help me anyway he could. But that had to be a last resort. Before doing that I'd just have to try all the businesses in town and see if anyone wanted help.

I looked up the beach and saw no one, then looked in the direction I'd come. Also no one. I was the only person on the entire beach. Then I remembered a photo I just saw in *Look* magazine of a beach in New York that was so covered with people, you could barely see the sand. Once again, I felt grateful for living here, where you could sit on a beach all alone and listen to the cry of the seagulls and let the rhythm of the waves soothe your soul, console you out of hopelessness. I watched a mother eagle glide into her nest on top of one of the mighty sea stacks, bringing food for her eaglet—a little ball of feathers with mouth agape—who was totally dependent on her. I looked at all these craggy geologic monuments in all different shapes and sizes, dotting the coastline here from the Cape all the way to Blacklock Point, providing refuge and safety to a variety of birds. As the waves crashed noisily against them, I felt their strength, their power. And I knew I would endure, even succeed. I wouldn't let my mother down.

Port Orford 1962

It had been a very busy day since we opened at 7 a.m., with all the locals coming in for breakfast, wanting their coffee and eggs, bacon, sausage, ham, toast—white, rye or wheat—and coffee, more coffee. It seemed a never-ending stream till almost noon. My feet were sore, my knees throbbing. All I could think of was to sit, take a break, have some water and just breathe. I worked that shift almost since the day Tom died, every day, six days a week, with Verna, who came in at 9—she had little kids to get off to school. We would double-team it until 2 when I got off and she stayed that last hour till 3 covering the late lunch crowd. CJ's was one of the few places you could get a full breakfast, all day, and it was good—fresh and reasonable—that's what drew the locals. But there were tourists and truckers passing through as well, many repeaters who knew the place as well as CJ, Verna and I.

We were like a family, each with our hopes and dreams, our fears and our sorrows. CJ used to drink—he liked his whiskey neat—but after so many years of lost jobs and drunken stupors, his wife left him, took his kid one night and stole away. He got a letter from her a year later saying she found a new man to love, one who didn't drink and treated her and their son real nice. She was never coming back. CJ went off on a binge, got into a brawl at the bar, wound up in jail, where the sheriff—who knew him since childhood—sent him to mandatory rehab. I guess you could say that was his bottom, cause after that, he got his life on track. He borrowed some money from his aunt and opened this place, where he's been clean and sober ever since. That was 10 years ago.

How different this place was from the CJ's of my youth. That place was mostly a bar that served burgers and the like to make it more respectable. But really, it was a saloon, the only one left in town that I remember, a place where men went to drink. Not long after I returned home from Portland, CJ closed up and left town, moved to Arizona for his health. Other than having the same initials, the two men were not family, but the original CJ was so well known along this corridor, frequently someone would ask my boss if they were related.

Verna came a year before me and her story was the reverse of CJ's. She was married for eight years to a drunken control freak, a man with lots of money, so she lived very well, in a suburb of Chicago. But he'd come home at night and start drinking and abusing her. At first, he was just domineering, but with time, the drinking and controlling became suffocating. Then he started slapping her, then punching her and she knew she had to get out or she would be dead, or worse yet, he would start on the kids. So, like CJ's wife, with the help of a friend, she ran away with her boy and girl who were four and seven, and took one bus after another, leapfrogging across the country, heading west until she ran out of country and found herself in Port Orford in a run-down room in a boarding house. She passed CJ's on her way to taking the kids to school and on her way back, she stopped to see if he needed any help. When he told her no, she started to cry out of desperation. He made her sit down and gave her a cup of coffee. Meanwhile, orders were backing up in the kitchen and he was trying to calm her, while she blurted her story out about her drunken husband. Once CJ heard that, I guess he figured helping her was part of his atonement, so he hired her part time, even though he had enough help and couldn't really afford her. But in time, the business grew and soon he needed her full time. Thanks to CJ, she got herself a little apartment for her and her kids, CJ got back his self-respect and I got a new best friend.

The lunch crowd starting coming in and the orders switched from eggs to burgers. The tables were filling up and so was the counter where I was working. I was hustling orders from the kitchen to customer, bringing extra cole slaw, coffee refills, more water, a side of mayo, when I noticed the last spot at the counter was occupied. I replaced the coffee pot and hustled down to the end to take his order. I'd never seen him before, so figured this was his first time here and offered him a menu. He declined, and looking up at the white board, said he'd have the special—a bacon cheeseburger—with a glass of milk. Milk. That got my attention. Men ordered root beer, lemonade, coffee, or water, but never milk. I must have shown my surprise because he asked, rather crankily, "What, you don't have milk?"

"Of course," I said smiling, to overcome his ire. "Coming right up." That was my first inkling that he was different, and not in the best of moods.

I hurried to the kitchen to place his order and pick up a plate for another customer. I gave him not another thought as I focused on serving the other patrons. It was still a busy day and I was doing my best to keep up with the flow and keep everyone happy. Soon, I picked up the bacon cheeseburger, stopped to fill a large glass of milk, and brought him both items. I asked if he needed anything else and he curtly said, no, he was good. I went on to the next order and the next and then started to supply dessert to those who wanted it and gave checks and coffee refills. Eventually, the place started to empty and it was a little after 1:30. I knew I would be leaving soon and couldn't wait to be sitting on my sofa with my feet up.

I asked the cranky man if he wanted dessert or coffee. He declined both, so I gave him his check. Before I could walk away, he said, "Here" and handed me a $20 bill. I couldn't get much of a read on him at all. He was rather unkempt, with a beard and longish hair, wearing a trucker hat and sunglasses. I took his money and went to get his change. While at the register, one of the locals was heading for the door. He said, "Thanks Jennifer, see you tomorrow." I told him to try to be good till then. He was one of the locals who made me feel so welcomed here. A former neighbor of mine, Ned was now a widower in his 60's and came in every day either for breakfast or lunch and was a warm, jovial man who always had a smile and a kind word. I took the change back and told the stranger to come in again, hoping he would say something about his being here today, but he said nothing. Just nodded, finished his milk, got up, picked up most of his change and walked out the door. I noticed then he was tall and lean, had a nice build. Too bad he was so cranky.

I cleared the counter, which was empty now and reset the places for the next crowd. I said goodbye to CJ and Verna, said I would see them tomorrow and left.

I went home and had a hot bath and relaxed a bit before the kids got home from school. We had a typical evening: homework, dinner, talking about our day, a little TV and soon it was time for bed. I locked up, checked on the kids and turned in. Tomorrow would be here soon enough.

The next few days passed in much the same way. The same schedule, same regulars, same cranky stranger. Each day I tried to give him an opening—a chance for him to tell me something about himself or how long he planned to be in town. But he revealed nothing. He interested me because he didn't fit the pattern. Usually when someone came in for 3 days or more, they weren't tourists—those you saw once, maybe twice. Four days in a row fit more with being a local, yet he didn't try to fit in or make friends. He kept to himself, eating his lunch and drinking his milk in silence. Verna even tried to get him talking by telling him he was becoming a regular, but he just nodded and kept eating. By the end of the week, we resigned ourselves to never knowing his story. Whether he came back again or not, he would remain a mystery.

The Saturday crowd was emptying out, including Ned, who called to me before going out the door. "Hey, Jennifer, I'm playing tonight at the Lamppost. Why don't you come on by? We start at 9."

"I don't know, Ned. Its pizza night with the kids and I can't give that up."

"Well, come by later, when the kids go to bed. We'll be there till midnight. I'd love for you to hear me play."

"Well, maybe. I'll see how it goes." He just stood there, waiting for me to say yes, so I acquiesced and said, "Maybe I'll see you later."

He took that as a yes and said, "Ok. See you later," and he was gone, out the door. I finished cleaning up before heading home for a fun night with the kids.

*

The pizza was gone and I had just come in from taking the box out to the trash. I sat on the couch and put my feet up. I was tired—it had been a busy week. The kids were tired, too. They were each involved in some kind of activity through school: football, basketball, baseball and gymnastics. Between the practices and games, they were always doing something. They were already in bed. I thought about Ned. I didn't want to disappoint him, but I was really beat. I was about to get up to go to bed myself, when I realized it was only 9 o'clock. I was too young to be going to bed at that hour. I went to check on the girls—they were sound asleep. Then I went to the boys' room. Jimmy was asleep but Tommy, my oldest, was awake, reading one of his favorite science-fiction books. I asked him how he would feel if I went out for an hour, to go listen to Ned play. He said, "Go ahead, Mom. I'm gonna be up for a while, in case anyone wakes up. Go. Have some fun." I promised I would be back in an hour and gave him a kiss on the forehead. He was such a great help to me, always pitching in. He was only 13, but very mature. He had assumed the role of man-of-the-family when Tom died.

I threw on a skirt and a frilly shirt, twisted up my hair in a clip, put on some lipstick and locked the door on the way out. The Lamppost was only two blocks down the hill, so I was there in no time. When I walked in, Ned and his friends were playing. There were quite a few people there, most all of whom I recognized. I waved to Ned and went to sit at the bar, between a couple of guys who frequented CJ's. I nodded hello to them and ordered a ginger ale. The music was very good. Ned was playing his guitar and singing a sad, old country-western song,

"Walkin' After Midnight." He was astonishingly good, I never would have imagined this grizzled old man would be so smooth on stage. I was enjoying the sound and the energy in the bar. People were kicking back and just having a good time. I was taking it all in and noticed a man with a trucker hat all the way down at the end of the bar on the last stool. It was him. Still had on the shades. He seemed to be just staring at his glass.

The song ended and Ned announced they were taking a break. He came over to me and gave me a hug. Said he was happy I came. I told him I was happy I came too and that I really liked his sound, that I thought he was good. He got all modest on me.

"That's an awfully sad song," I said.

"Oh, it doesn't make me sad. It was my wife's favorite song, and whenever I sing it, I remember her singing or humming it and that makes me happy. I'm sorry if it made you sad."

"Don't worry about it, I'm glad it makes you happy." I went on to tell him I wouldn't be staying long, that Tommy was watching the other kids and that I didn't want to leave him too long. I promised to stay for one more song before ducking out, which I did.

I hadn't gone very far out on the street, when I heard my name being called. I turned and was surprised to see the stranger.

He was coming toward me and asked, "Would it be alright if I walked you home."

My caution kicked on. "No. I'm sorry, I don't know you," I responded. There was no way I was going to lead a man I didn't know to my home and my kids. I had tried all week to befriend him, to no avail, and now here he was acting like an old friend.

"But you do know me," he said as he removed his hat and sunglasses and pushed his hair back from his face. In the light of the neon sign, I could see his face, but he didn't look familiar to me at all.

"I'm sorry, but I don't recognize you," I said, trying to remember if I'd ever seen his face.

"Well, it's been awhile. You look exactly like I remember you, only prettier," he added.

Now I was embarrassed that I couldn't remember him. "You have me at a disadvantage. You know my name, but I don't know yours."

"Jack Long," he said as he walked toward me.

It was as if a giant gong went off in my head. I remembered him. Jack Long. One of the men rescued from the torpedoed ship twenty years ago. The one with the blue eyes, which I couldn't see in the dark. "Well, I'm glad to see you survived the war," I managed to say in my bewilderment, as he took my hand and looked down into my eyes.

"I did, thanks to you," he said with the warmest smile.

"Why didn't you tell me who you were at CJ's? You were being so cranky and wearing a disguise, why?" I asked, completely baffled by this turn of events.

"I guess I wasn't sure I was ready to reveal myself to you. Not sure you would be friendly toward me. But after seeing you tonight, talking to that old guy, with your beautiful smile, I figured it was safe," he said, with a smile.

I was still rather perplexed by this explanation, but said, "I'm not sure Ned would appreciate your calling him an 'old guy' and I don't really understand why you would think I wouldn't be friendly toward you. You're the one who left without saying goodbye."

"I know, and I'm sorry I left the way I did, but I really had no choice in the matter. I have regretted that for years. And as to the other thing, I guess that's kind of a long story." He paused, then continued, "Come on, let me walk you, I already know where you live."

My radar went off then, "Have you been following me?" I asked, trying hard not to panic.

"No. But it's part of the long story. Why don't you come back inside and I'll tell you?" he asked.

"I'd love to, but I can't. I left my kids at home and I have to get back." I was totally confused by this whole conversation and I really wanted to hear his story, so I offered, "Since you know where I live," I said with emphasis, "Why don't you come for breakfast tomorrow? 9 o'clock."

"OK, but are you sure you don't want me to walk you?" he asked.

"No, I can go faster alone. I'll see you tomorrow morning. And bring your appetite," I said, as I dashed off.

When I got home, Tommy was asleep, as were the other three. I locked up and went to my bedroom, got ready for bed. All the while, my mind was a flurry of thoughts, memories and questions. I had to work at calming my anxiousness. Eventually I fell asleep, wondering what tomorrow would bring.

*

I woke to the sound of bird song and sunny rays warming my face. . .and I didn't hear any wind. Maybe it was going to be one of those rare, wonderfully beautiful days. I got up and dressed, taking a little extra care, remembering that we were having a guest for breakfast. When I got downstairs, the kids were up and dressed, starting to get things ready for Sunday breakfast. This was the one day of the week, when we could spend some quality time together, with a big breakfast, usually pancakes. There was no school, no sports, no work, just us and all the time we wanted together. The boys were busy mixing the pancake batter so I told them to make extra, that we were having company for breakfast. An old friend of mine, I told them, which started a barrage of questions. I told them his name and that I knew him during the war and that they would have to wait for him to arrive to find out anything more.

I had just finished putting the coffee on—wondering if he drank coffee, since he drank milk for lunch—and there was a knock on the door. I went to the door and there he was, so much more like I remembered him. He was nicely dressed, clean-shaven, and his sun-drenched hair was slicked back—no sunglasses, no hat, just a very handsome man holding a bunch of beautiful flowers. I opened the screen door and said, "Welcome." He entered and thrust the flowers toward me, saying "Good Morning, Jenny." I accepted the bunch and said, "They're lovely, thank you. Come on in and meet my children." We entered the kitchen and the kids had stopped what they were doing and stood like statues. "Kids, this is Jack Long, who I

106

met here in Port Orford during the war." I went on to introduce Jack to each of them. They each smiled and went back to their work. I told him, "It will be a few minutes before breakfast is ready, so please have a seat, there at the end of the table. Can I bring you some coffee, or juice? Or some milk?" "Coffee would be great. Black," he said with a smile. "I'll get it, Mom." It was Mary, who was looking completely star-struck. We'd never had a guest for breakfast or any meal for that matter, let alone a man, a handsome man at that. She brought his mug of coffee, which he politely thanked her for. "Mom, the batter's ready," Tommy called to me. "If you'll excuse me, I'll get pancakes started," I said. He nodded and offered to help, but I declined his offer. I told the kids to go sit with him and ask him what they wanted to know. I heard Tommy ask, "So how did you meet my mom?" and got busy in the kitchen.

When I returned to the dining room with a big tray of hot cakes and sausages, Jack was telling about manning the gun on the tanker, trying to hit the submarine that had torpedoed his ship. The kids were listening avidly, mouths agape. They'd never met anyone who'd fired a big gun like that. I handed Jack the platter of pancakes and Tommy, who was next to him, the sausages. They helped themselves and passed the platters on till everyone was served. I went to get some coffee for myself, then helped myself to the food. There were many more questions about the incident, which Jack didn't seem to mind. "Mom, why didn't you ever tell us there was a ship torpedoed here?" Jimmy was asking me.

"Well, we never really talked about the war. You didn't seem to be interested in your Uncle Frank's time in the service, so I didn't think to bring it up," I said by way of an explanation.

"Yeah, but Uncle Frank never shot a big gun like that," Jimmy said in his defense.

"Your uncle no doubt had some harrowing experiences of his own and might not have wanted to talk about it, or didn't want to seem like he was bragging," Jack interjected. "The war took a personal toll on every man and woman who served, some worse than others. I don't normally talk about it at all, except that is how I met you mother," he said as he smiled at me and I saw his beautiful blue eyes, those eyes that had haunted me for years.

We finished up our food and one by one, the kids vanished. On bikes and skates, going to a friend's house or to the park, the playground, or the beach, their usual Sunday haunts to just have fun.

When we were alone, I couldn't contain my curiosity any longer and asked, "So, why don't you tell me how it is you knew where I lived and why you are here?"

"Gladly," he said, "But why don't I help you clean up first."

"Alright," I said and we started clearing the table, taking dishes to the sink. I had every intention of letting them soak till he was gone, but he asked, "Do you want to wash or dry?"

"I'll wash," I said, completely surprised—Tom had never once offered to help with the dishes. As I washed and he dried, he asked me about the kids, their ages and what they liked to do, if they were good In school, sports. He seemed genuinely interested, not stalling for time. When he'd dried the last dish, I thanked him and said, "Let's sit in the living room, where it's more comfortable." I led the way and he followed. We sat on opposite ends of the sofa, facing each other, and I said, "You were just about to explain some things to me."

"Yes, I guess I was." And he paused. "Well, let me answer your first question first." Again, he paused, pensively.

"The reason I knew where you lived is because I actually own this house. I am your benefactor," he said in all seriousness. He stopped, seeing the surprised look on my face. "I guess I need to go back further in time, since you probably are wondering how I knew you needed a place to live."

"Well, yes, among other things," I said, somewhat annoyed.

He hesitated before saying, "You're special to me, Jenny. I guess I've known that since the first time I saw you, from that first time I opened my eyes and there you were, my angel, so sweet, so innocent, so gentle. Not like anyone I'd met before or since."

I sat there in disbelief; It was all so preposterous, so I asked, "If I was so special, why haven't you come back to me before now?"

"I did," he blurted, "but by that time, I was drinking pretty heavily, going down a wrong road. One morning I woke up in a strange bed and had no idea how I had gotten there. I had blacked out. I knew if I didn't stop drinking like that, I would be dead soon. I knew I needed help. I thought of you. How you had saved me. You mattered so much to me that I got sober and came up here. But my bad luck held out. I got here the day of your wedding. I actually saw you get married. I stood in the shadows, in the trees and watched and felt so desolate. You looked so pretty. . .and happy."

I was shocked and confused and even felt a bit betrayed. "But why didn't you make yourself known. Why didn't you show your face? I would have stopped the wedding for you. You and I only spent a few hours together, but I knew you were different. You say I was special to you, well, I felt the same way about you. I felt something for you I never felt for

Tom. Somewhere deep inside me, I knew you were everything to me that Tom wasn't."

"I couldn't. I couldn't do that to you. I was too messed up. I just ran back to LA and the bottle," he said as he turned to look out the window. He seemed so sad, so alone. I reached over and placed my hand on his, which he quickly took up and held tight.

"So much changed after leaving here in '42. I was mad as hell when the Navy showed up to take me from here. They took me to Oak Knoll Naval Hospital down in Oakland where they treated me for many weeks. And with each day, my anger grew. When I finally recovered from my burns, and was discharged, I was filled with rage. I felt anger for my crew mates who died, anger for feeling so helpless behind that gun waiting for the enemy to surface, which he never did. Anger for the pain he had caused me. I decided I wanted to get even on a much more level playing field. I wanted to be able to pull that trigger and know that I had actually killed my enemy. So, I became a pilot. I had flown some as a civilian, with my dad, so flight training was easier for me. I just had to learn the plane, which I did in a matter of months. By June of '43, I was on a carrier off an atoll in the South Pacific, making bombing runs on the Japanese fleet. Every time I shot down an enemy plane, I felt my anger subside. I was getting revenge for my lost mates."

I was listening raptly to him, trying to remember that time. June of '43, I was in Portland, at the hospital, might have even been thinking of him, wondering where he was.

"It was a fierce battle, lasted three days. The Marines were on the ground trying to take back the island from the Japanese and every time they wanted to advance, we fly boys were called on to distract the enemy and try to destroy their fire power. It was the last day and we had killed or driven off most of the enemy. I was about to head back to base when I got hit—a kamikaze came out of nowhere and strafed my plane. I lost all control—I was going down—so I parachuted out, and dropped into the sea. The Japanese ships were off in the distance but I could see land, so figured I could swim to shore. But the Japs were leaving the island, heading to their ships, when they spotted me and picked me up. I became their prisoner."

I remembered what the returning POW's had looked like and the stories they told, and could only imagine what he had been through. I could see his anguish and said, "You don't have to tell me the rest. Not now anyway."

He was visibly upset, so I moved closer and put my arm around him and held him close, with his head on my shoulder. "That's all in the past. You are fine now," I said, trying to console him. We sat like that for some time, when he lifted his head to look at me.

"I am fine now, that I am with you," he said as he looked in my eyes. We held each other's gaze; I was lost in the blueness of his eyes when he kissed me. His lips were warm and sensuous; I felt all my inhibitions melting away and I was being pulled down into a pool of long-buried desire, immersed in the sensation of the kiss, falling deeper and deeper into the abyss of yearning. Though I barely knew him, had spent so little time with him, I felt safe and connected in a way I had never felt with a man. I wanted him. His hand was on my breast, searching for a way inside my blouse, to the pulsing flesh inside. I opened my shirt to let him in. I wanted to feel his hands on my skin. At last he was there, cupping my breast and caressing me. Then his mouth was there, his hot tongue toying with me. I was on fire and wanted him as I had never wanted any man before. He pushed me gently down on the couch and lifted my skirt. I helped him take off my panties and unbutton his pants. He was hard and erect and soon slipped inside me, where he moved ever so gently, all the while kissing my lips and massaging my breasts. He was plunging rhythmically deeper and I was rising to meet his thrust. I was hungry for him and moaning with pleasure, like I had never known. We were rocking madly and I felt myself climbing higher and higher, till at once I screamed with wild abandon as I crested the top. I felt him shudder as he groaned with his own ecstasy and then fall limp on top of me, all the tension gone from our bodies. We lay there for a few moments before reality sunk in and I said frantically, "We best get decent before one of my kids pops in here." We laughed and hurriedly put ourselves back in order.

"Well I guess we got to know each other pretty quickly," he said jokingly.

"Yeah, I guess we did," I responded giddily. I was filled with a jumble of feelings. High, like I imagine the feeling a drug would induce, and also calm from the sexual release. I felt a closeness to this man who was a stranger, with whom I'd shared the most intimate connection. The pleasure with him was greater than anything I'd experienced with Tom—I never knew that sex could be so pleasurable.

He put his arms around me and drew me to him. We stood there holding each other, saying nothing, but feeling the heat passing between us. Like me, I suspect he was feeling a variety of emotions. Swamped by a wave of confusion, I broke the spell and drew away from him, saying, "Why don't we get some fresh air. It's a beautiful day and we should enjoy it." I led the way outside, across the lawn to a bench overlooking the ocean.

"I love sitting here by the sea," I said finally, not wanting to talk about what had just happened. I wasn't sure where we could go from here. I was confused to the point of not knowing what the natural next step would or should be.

He reached for my hand and holding it, he said, "Why don't you come to LA with me? I have a big house, large enough for you and the kids—they can each have their own room. And there's a pool and a tennis court. The kids would love it there. You'd like it too, no more working so hard. And, you and I can be together, we can be married, as we should have been all these years."

He sat there looking happy and excited, no doubt expecting me to say yes, yes, yes. But I couldn't. I couldn't imagine the life he was suggesting. Beside the fact that I hadn't seen him in twenty years, and barely knew him then, I couldn't think about leaving this town for good—this was my home. He was a special man and I felt I could love him completely. I was sure the kids could love him too, but this was too great a leap to take. To get to know a new man, a new home, a city, a lifestyle was all too much for me right now. I had never been an impulsive person and couldn't start now.

"I can't do that, Jack. I can't leave this town and this life. Not for me, not for my kids. I appreciate what you are offering, and I'll admit, I have strong feelings for you. I truly like you and would love to spend more time getting to know you better and can even imagine marrying you and spending the rest of my life with you, but I can't leave here." His face showed his dejection and disbelief. I tried to select my words carefully and went on. "I don't expect you to understand that. I'm sure you think this is a little hick town that no one would ever choose to live in—a retreat, a place for a quick visit to recharge your batteries. But this is a community and my home, a place where everyone is connected and reliant on one another. It's a wholesome place where my kids are safe and growing up with good values, breathing clean, fresh air. And yes, life is hard in this little town. So many die just trying to make a living, to support their families. The fishermen who say goodbye to their wives in the morning, and just never come back. We've lost so many fathers, husbands, brothers, sons. They get tossed overboard or the whole boat gets swamped and they all drown. You know very well how hungry the sea can be. Then there are the loggers. Men like my husband, who get hit with runaway logs, practically ripping them in two. Or the ones who get hit in the head with a tree on a haul line and die from a brain hemorrhage, or get decapitated driving the truck when the logs shift. These are dangerous jobs and nobody gets rich. If the men don't get killed, they get hurt or maimed. They suffer broken bones, lose fingers, hands, arms. But they do it because their fathers and grandfathers did it. Or because they have no other option with a limited education. They do it for family. They do it because they want to stay here and raise their kids in a safe place, so they can grow up with decent values, with good neighbors who will always be there for them. They. . .we want to be part of a nurturing community. That's why I can't leave. This town is my home. Even though I have to work hard and still can't give my kids all that they want, we are a family with lots of love. I stay here for my kids.

"My brother left town right after the war. Went to Portland to go to college on the government's dime. Married a girl from there, became an engineer, started a business, had a couple of kids, a fancy house and lots of *things*. He seemed happy. Now, he drinks too much, his wife divorced him and his kids are in trouble a lot, either with the school or the police. So, I think for all the hardness of life here, it's still the best place to be, especially for my kids, at least while they are growing up. I'm sorry. I can't think about myself and my own happiness, I have to think about them."

We sat there, looking at each other, both of us sad, searching each other's face for what seemed like minutes. At last, he said, "Wow. That's probably why I love you. You have such strong feelings, and strong values, and are pretty selfless." He paused and took my hand in both of his. "You know, when I got back from the war, from the POW camp, I was filled with loathing, for myself, my captors, the lost years of my life. I took up drinking and I was pretty good at it. I drank every day and got stinking drunk every night. I met a woman who liked to drink as much as I did and married her. We spent two years together in a state of blissful inebriation until I came home one day and found a man in bed with her. So, that was the end of that. I went back to being a lone drunk. Till I ran into this Admiral I knew pretty well. He managed to give me a little of my self-respect back, got me to stop drinking and helped me start a charter flight business in Hollywood. I made some connections at the studios and before I knew it, my business was booming. I was flying movie stars and directors back and forth to movie sets. . .it was great. Then I remembered you and how I enjoyed being around you and decided to come up here to find you. That's when I watched you get married and started feeling sorry for myself again.

"I went back to the bottle, hooked up with a starlet and continued in my downward spiral, but out of respect for the Admiral, I only drank at night. I managed to keep the business going, even thriving, while I drowned my sorrows every night. Eventually, the starlet left, which I didn't blame her for. I was glad she got away from me. I continued to run my business by day and drink by night. I watched the degradation of society in the back of my plane—the drugs, the booze, the sex, people using each other for fame. But I was making money, lots of it. I kept expanding the business and then had three planes. I was still drinking hard though and it was showing. I was bloated, my face was red and I felt crappy all the time. I had to go for a physical for my pilot's license and the doctor told me if I didn't quit drinking, I'd be dead soon. It was a wakeup call. I went to rehab, got sober and healthy and on a lark, flew back up here. I checked up on you and you seemed happy, still married, with four kids. I was happy for you. This house had recently burned down, so I bought it and had it renovated. I stayed here a few times and felt good whenever I was here. I relished the quiet, the clean air. So, I know exactly what you're talking about. I completely understand why you wouldn't want to leave here and why you wouldn't want to live in LA. I truly do," he said with resignation.

I smiled at him and felt so much respect for his courage and his honesty and told him so.

"I don't know how courageous I was. It was just survival. I survived the camp, and the prison of the bottle. But I know after spending this day together, the only way I can continue to survive is with you in my life. Once again, I feel like you've rescued me. I feel. . .inspired. Hopeful. And maybe this is a crazy idea, but even though we can't move to the same location, I think we can still have a relationship. We can stay connected on the phone and I can continue to fly up here every now and then so we can be together, make a life together, if that's okay with you. I know there is no other woman I want in my life and I am hoping you feel the same about me."

"It's more than okay with me," I said as I threw my arms around him and hugged him tight. I drew back then, remembering this wasn't just about me. "But if you want to be with me, you will have to be with my kids. You will have to be a part of their lives, as well."

"I never really thought about having kids. I was such a screw up, taking care of myself was enough of a challenge. But I like your kids—they're great. They just prove my instincts about you are right." He stopped and reached for my hands. "I can't promise you I can be a good father, but I can certainly be a good uncle."

Just then I saw Amy riding her bike up the hill, heading our way. "Good enough," I said as I gave him a quick kiss on the lips. "And here's your chance to start."

*

I woke up Monday morning, thinking about yesterday, what an incredible surprise it had been. It was a day of firsts: having a man in our home, one who was interested enough in us to hold a conversation; who related to the kids on each of their levels; and then to be made love to, that was the biggest surprise of all. I was still feeling dreamy, like a princess in a fairy tale, wrapped in a cocoon of love—a sense I had never known before, one of being desired, embraced, even treasured. I wanted to hold on to it for as long as possible, but then an inkling of guilt crept in. I had had sex with a man who wasn't my husband, which was against the behavior engrained in me. But he could have been my husband and could I dare to hope that he would be my husband one day. Besides, this was 1962. Societal rules and codes of morality were loosening. I'd even read something about a "love-in" back east. Furthermore, I was a grown woman and there was no chance I would become pregnant.

I thought about his asking me to go to LA and my response. Was I wrong, was it just my unwillingness to take a chance, my lack of adventurousness? Was I preventing myself from having a wonderful relationship with an extraordinary man, who might be the father my children needed and deserved? Did I not think I deserved it? Or was I right about all the reasons I had given Jack for wanting to stay here? I thought again about life here. Besides the forests and the sea, which provided fresh local fish, it was bucolic with numerous farms and ranches just outside the town limit, that provided a wealth of natural, chemical-free food. We could pick fresh blueberries in the summer and buy local meats and fresh-picked produce

118

practically year-round: Cranberries, farm-fresh eggs, grass-fed bacon, beef, milk—even grow some of our own food in the community garden plot. On top of that we could do our own fishing for fresh, plump, wild salmon and steelhead trout in the crystal clear, clean rivers throughout fall and winter.

I looked at the clock and realized I was going to be late. I jumped out of bed, dressed as fast as I could, kissed my kids who were getting ready for school and ran out the door.

CJ's had the usual breakfast crowd of locals and we were busy as ever. I had lots of energy, feeling much like that 18-year-old girl anticipating the Saturday night dance. I was continuing to think about the day before, how Jack had spent the afternoon with me and the kids as they drifted home one by one. He took us all out for fish and chips, the local culinary specialty, which was a real treat for the kids, as we never had money to eat out. They had lots of questions and he had lots of patience. It was a fairy-tale experience, everyone so happy. The kids were enthralled with his stories of flying and planes, especially the boys, but Mary and Amy were just as rapt, anxious to hear about the movie stars he'd met. I couldn't remember a single incidence like it with Tom. I was still pinching myself to make sure it had really happened.

I was hopping around CJ's taking orders and delivering food with a spring in my step and a big smile on my face. Verna passed me in the kitchen and said, "You must have had a good weekend, I've never seen you with so much energy." I smiled back at her and said, "I had a remarkable weekend. I'll tell you about it later," and dashed off with three orders of eggs.

I was at the counter, refilling coffee cups when Sheriff Johnson came in. He nodded to me and went to talk to a couple of fishermen down at the end. They were having a serious conversation, but I went down there anyway to see if the Sheriff wanted a seat or any food. He said no, that he was on duty; he was here to tell these men that one of the fishing boats, the *Betty-Sue*, was long overdue and that they were having no luck reaching them on the radio. The Coast Guard had been called out to search for them and there was a group of wives and fishermen down at the wharf holding vigil, waiting for some word. They got up to leave and I told them I would be down there as soon as I finished my shift. I knew the families of the men who were on that boat, so I wanted to be there to offer any support I could.

The mood in CJ's turned very somber as news of the missing boat spread from table to table. This wasn't the first time this had happened and we all knew it wouldn't be the last. All too often, boats went missing and it was rare for them to be found and rescued. But sometimes, there was a busted engine and a broken radio. . .it had happened once or twice.

I finished up my shift and went down to the dock. There were quite a few people there, standing around, waiting for news, any news. I searched out the wives of the three men from the boat. They were huddled together, with fear and anxiety etched on their faces. I greeted each one with a hug, which they returned, and told them I was there for them. The four of us stood together, holding hands for the next couple of hours. I listened intently as they told stories of their husbands, things they'd done, mostly happy times, and things they wanted to do. Other women came by, as did fishermen as they brought their boats in, filled with their catch. Soon their kids came down to join them—school was out. I excused myself and ran up the hill to make sure my kids were okay and to let them know where I was. I got them settled in with homework and left chili for them to heat up for dinner. I told them I would be back before bedtime and ran back down the hill.

The hours dragged on with no word. The weather was changing. Dark clouds on the horizon were moving our way and soon the drizzle came. Waves were pelting the jetty and crashing over the top. Another storm was rolling in. The wind picked up and the drizzle turned to rain. It was getting nasty out, when Sheriff Johnson got out of his car and announced that he'd just heard from the Coast Guard: they were suspending the search due to the weather, but would get back out there at first light, assuming the weather improved. I don't think I will ever forget the look on the wives' faces. They were distraught and bleak, beginning to falter in their hope and optimism; my heart bled for them. The Sheriff and a few of the other men offered to drive the families home. They didn't want to go, but knew they had to get their kids home out of the weather. I hugged each of them as they left and started my trek home. Ned offered me a lift which I accepted, anxious to get out of the rain and home as quickly as possible.

I got inside just as the storm turned violent. I locked up and went to put on dry clothes. When I came out of my room, the kids were all there waiting for me, wanting to know the latest news. They each knew children from those families and were concerned. Amy was particularly upset; her best friend was the daughter of one of the men. I comforted her as best I could and told her and the others to remain optimistic and say their prayers that the boat would be found with the men alive. We all went to bed, though I wasn't sure how well any of us would sleep.

Life went on the next day, people following their routines, many just going through the motions, waiting for word, any word, good or bad, just wanting to know. CJ cooked up a bunch of eggs, meats and pancakes and we packed it up for the families. A few of the guys delivered it. The weather had improved so we knew the Coast Guard would be out searching.

We kept working, trying to stay busy and thankfully there was a steady stream of customers, mostly tourists, to keep us occupied and not dwelling on the tragedy at hand. We all knew, the longer it went on, the less likely they would be found afloat and alive.

It was a little after 12 when Sheriff Johnson walked in looking stern and we all stopped doing what we were doing to hear what he had to say. As we all dreaded, he announced they had found debris in the water about 125 miles out including a body and a flotation ring from the *Betty Sue* and that a continuous search had turned up nothing further. They were coming in so the body could be identified. CJ announced we would be closing early, for everyone to finish up, but no one wanted to eat. They all just cashed out and left, as did we, quickly cleaning up.

I headed down to the dock and it seemed everyone from CJ's and half the town had done the same. I stood with the wives, which now was a group of about 30—The Port Orford Fishery Wives—all women married to fishermen who banded together to offer help and support to one another during times of loss. They were a strong bunch of women who suffered untold hardships. When their men couldn't get out to fish due to the weather or illness or severe injury or a damaged boat, they still had hungry mouths to feed. When their men were out to sea for long periods of time, they had to be both mother and father to their children. And every time they kissed them goodbye, there was the possibility they would never see them again. . .alive. You had to be hardy to marry a fisherman, and that's why they stuck together. They were all of the same breed, all subject to the same quirks of fate. I admired them greatly and so now stood with them, to let them know I cared, that I empathized with them. One of the three women was going to have a body to bury, the other two would not, but either way, they each had lost the man they loved, the man who provided for them and their children. Life would never be the same.

*

It was one of those magical summer days on the Oregon coast, one that comes along every now and then—warm, sunny, and no wind. We were together as a family cavorting on the beach: Mary and I looking for agates and beach glass, Jack helping Amy build a sand castle, Tommy and Jimmy playing in the surf. Like living in a postcard, not one of us had a care in the world. Jack had flown up last night for the long weekend, as he had done several times before. He and I were growing closer and were clearly in love. Each time we'd been alone together was a special time, filled with tender moments, the sharing of innermost secrets and mutually satisfying love-making. And, perhaps most importantly, the children had all accepted him as more than just my friend and relished the time they spent with him. He made each one of them feel special, always seeming to know just how to connect with them, whether boy or girl. He was so much more than I could have asked for in a man, he was "beyond my wildest dreams" to be cliché. I stood there on the beach, watching him and feeling so blessed to have him in my life.

The tide was low and the boys were running back and forth through the tunnel in Battle Rock which was only accessible when the tide was out. Tommy was calling to Jack to come see what they'd found. He stood up and I sat there admiring his body, tall and lean and already nicely tanned, except for those areas on his body where he'd been burned— they were white where all the pigment had been burned out. Despite that, he was very nice to look at. He jogged over to the tunnel and disappeared inside with them. I went back to reading my book with Mary beside me, soaking up the sun, "working on her tan," as she said. Suddenly, Tommy was calling me, frantically running toward me. "What's the matter, Tommy," I asked in a panic.

"It's Jack, Mom. He staggered out of the cave and he doesn't look right," he said as we ran down to the opening of the tunnel. There was Jack, sitting in the sand, white as a sheet, staring off to the horizon. "Jack, what's wrong? Are you alright?" I said as I scanned his body. He didn't seem to be hurt, but he didn't answer me, just looked off into space. I shook him and called his name. Eventually, his eyes focused on me. "Jack, are you alright?" I asked as calmly as I could. "Tell me what happened." By this time, Tommy, Jimmy, Mary and Amy were standing around me, looking just as concerned. After what seemed like minutes, Jack finally looked around at all the faces staring at him and said, "I'm alright. Can we go sit in the sun?"

Tommy and I helped him up and walked him back to the blanket. He assured us all he was okay and told the kids to go back to playing, he just wanted to rest, and not to worry about him. He seemed to be back to his old self, the color returning to his skin, but I could tell he was rattled. Since this was so out of character for him, I needed to know what had happened, so I asked him again.

He sat there looking at his hands, which were clenched together. Finally, he said, "When I walked into that tunnel, I was transported back to one of the camps in Japan. I was back in the caves where they kept us. Cold, hungry, wounded, convinced I was going to die."

"Oh, Jack. I'm so sorry. I never knew you were in a cave or I would have told the boys."

"It's not your fault or theirs. I guess all these years I've managed to avoid being in a cave. Today, I just forgot. I never wanted to think about it. . .to remember."

"Do you want to talk about it now, now that you're safe and free?"

On that sunny, friendly beach in the fresh air, consoled by the rhythmic sound of the waves hitting the shore, he proceeded to tell me about the horrors of his 15-month captivity. He was a *honoi,* a captive, a class lower than prisoner of war. There was no record of them, their captivity was not reported to the U.S., so as far as anyone was concerned, they were MIA. He told me about the constant beatings, the endless questioning, the starvation, wearing nothing but rags that left him shivering in the winter, having to stand at attention for hours, or working countless hours in a coal mine, manually digging and hauling coal to a ship, black with coal dust in his eyes, nose and mouth. He painted a horrible picture of insufferable torture and cruelty, but yet he survived with many others. He attested to the endurance of the human spirit and the unbreakable will to survive. I felt almost ashamed that while he had been hopelessly suffering, I was safe and well-fed in a comfortable home in Portland. I remembered the stories I had heard from the returning POW's in the hospital and I felt the same shame and guilt then for them. But all during the war, we had no idea what was happening to thousands of our men, no inkling of the barbarism and brutality they were being subjected to.

"When I was freed, I started to drink to cover up my memories. With enough alcohol in me, I didn't have to think about it. . .it wasn't real, just a bad dream. With all my back pay, I stayed numb for years until I ran into that Admiral. The rest of the story you know."

He sat there looking deflated, like a shadow of himself. I put my arms around him and caressed him to me. "Thank you for telling me. I know that wasn't easy to relive." I felt his body relax as the present returned to his being. I kissed his temple and told him, "I know you know this, but at this point, that camp is just a memory, a distant memory. It is part of your history, and helped to define the wonderful man you have become. You are here with me and the kids who love you. You are successful and healthy and strong. Your captors have no power over you anymore."

He looked at me and smiled, broke from my embrace, got up and ran into the freezing-cold ocean, and just as quickly ran back out. "Damn, that water is cold," he exclaimed as he plopped back down on the blanket, making sure to drip cold water on me. We all laughed that he would do such a crazy thing and went back to having a glorious day on the beach.

Port Orford 1963

We were largely unaffected by so much of what happened around the country. There were no civil rights "sit-ins," because there were no negroes in Port Orford. In fact, there were very few in the whole state as a result of the discriminatory black exclusion clause in the state's constitution, barring blacks from owning property or making contracts. Though never enforced, and eventually rescinded, the law was shamefully effective in keeping blacks from our state.

Also, there were no angry college students demonstrating here—we were hundreds of miles away from the nearest college. We only read about these things in the weekly newspaper. But war, that was the only national event we could not seem to escape. Now it was Vietnam, another faraway place we knew nothing about. . .not even where it was. But we soon learned, sadly, we learned. Our new, young President was sending troops—the Green Berets as they were known—to this place we'd never heard of, to fight communism. It was like Korea all over again. The Communist North against the Democratic South. Truman's Doctrine persisted. Would we be fighting the spread of Communism forever? Thank God, my boys were too young. I just hoped this war would be over before they turned eighteen.

But all too soon, it was déjà vu. We were at war. Our President was dead—albeit not from natural causes—and our Vice President was thrust into a situation not of his making. This community was isolated from the rest of the country in so many ways, on so many issues, but we could not escape our deep sense of loss for the cruel and untimely death of our esteemed President. School closed, as did all businesses, including CJ's, as we, like the rest of the country, sat glued to the TV, watching with great sadness, crying, as the President was laid to rest, with his wife and young children bravely looking on. We saw the dream of Camelot shatter, replaced by the underlying dread that we would again be forced to give up young men that we knew and loved.

Jack had been here the prior weekend, flying up as he did at least once a month. He called to offer to come back, to mourn with us, but I knew he had a busy week and told him to stay put, that we were fine, just sad. When CJ's finally opened, the mood was much more somber and subdued, not much laughter or guys joking around. . .it was hard to be upbeat with so much uncertainty. As the days and weeks passed, the town slipped back into its old rhythm, though decidedly more sluggish, like moving through molasses. It was December and we were dealing with winter storms, the latest of which washed lumber and a storage container off the dock into the harbor. A pall hung over the whole town—the whole country—but Christmas was coming, and still had to be celebrated for the sake of the children.

With Jack in my life, I was planning a quiet, yet festive, holiday with him and the kids. Our memories of Christmas over the last ten years or so hadn't been that great. Tom had been gone for the last four years and for many years before that he was mostly drunk. The onus for our family Christmas celebration had fallen solely on me, to provide a decorated tree, presents *and* the dinner. For once, it was nice to have a man in our lives who wanted to participate in that. Jack had grilled me about each of the kids, wanting to get the perfect gift for each one and was coming up two days early to pick out a tree. I was excited about it, but I think the kids were looking forward to it more than I. Though Jack wasn't here a lot of the time, he was making them feel like they had a father who loved them.

*

It was late and I sat in my room wrapping the last of the presents I had for the kids. Jack was coming tomorrow and the plan was to take the kids into the forest to find and chop down a Christmas tree, something they'd never done before. Jack was so great at teaching the kids things they never knew or experienced before. He'd taken them so many great places they'd never been. Like last Memorial Day when Jack took us all down to Brookings to attend the Azalea Festival. Not to see Azaleas, but to meet the man who had been on the submarine responsible for Jack's burns. He had read the article just as I had about Nobuo Fujita coming from Japan to celebrate the 20th anniversary of the Brookings bombing, which he had perpetrated. That is a day I don't think I will ever forget.

We were getting ready to leave for the drive south and I had just walked downstairs to see how the kids were doing, when Jack came out of the bathroom dressed in his uniform. I had never seen him in uniform before and he was mesmerizing—stunning in his dress uniform regalia. He stood there looking so tall and trim and handsome in the navy-blue suit with a white hat tucked under his arm. I went to stand in front of him, enthralled by the gold buttons, colorful ribbons and medals pinned to his chest. "Wow," was all I could manage to say. Just then both the boys and girls came flying out of their rooms, chomping to get going, and stopped in their tracks, at the sight of Jack. They were just as literate as I, with their "wows" and "holy cows." None of us really knew what to do, should we salute or bow, because he sure looked like royalty.

He broke the spell, by saying, "It's just a uniform, a suit really. But I wanted to wear it for the ceremony. I'm hoping I have the chance to meet him as a final act of closure."

"Alright then, let's be on our way, so we're not late," I said and corralled the kids out and into the car.

It was a beautiful day, sunny and warm. The drive down the coast was spectacular, the sunlight glinting off the water and the amazing rock formations strewn here and there offshore. It was incredible that at my age, I'd never driven south and was captivated by the scenery. Jack was telling the kids what he knew about Fujita and how he had launched this little light airplane on the deck of the same submarine that was believed to have torpedoed the tanker he was on. Fujita had flown inland over the forest and dropped two incendiary bombs hoping to start a forest fire. But fortunately, there had been a lot of rain prior to his flight and the trees and ground cover were saturated, so didn't ignite.

We arrived in Brookings just as the parade was finishing up and people started to gather in Azalea Park where the ceremony was to be held. As we walked toward the stage, a woman approached Jack and said she was one of the organizers and asked if he wanted to join the other veterans on the stage. He started to say no, that he wanted to stay with his family—and oh, how my heart soared to hear him use that word—but I urged him to go, telling him we would love to see him on the stage. The kids were nodding their agreement, so he conceded and went with her. Jack took his place behind a man in a wheelchair, after greeting him and shaking his hand. There were quite a few veterans there of varying ages, from their 60's to 30's, from World Wars I and II and Korea. A few had on their uniforms; others, just a hat that identified in which war they had fought and survived, but none was as striking as Jack.

The high school band started to play "The Star-Spangled Banner" as we saluted the American Flag set on the stage. At once, I was feeling patriotic, in a way I hadn't felt in 20 years, filled with pride and honor, especially seeing the veterans before me. When the song was finished, several men walked onto the stage including a Japanese man I assumed was Nobuo Fujita. He was carrying something in his hands wrapped in a red silk cloth. One man, who was the mayor, walked to the podium as the others were seated behind him, and began his speech. He recounted the events of 20 years ago, and the knowledge that was later revealed of the man who had actually flown the plane that dropped those bombs. He told of a city council meeting over a year ago, when someone suggested inviting this man to Brookings as a gesture of peace between our two nations. He spoke of the complicated efforts to gain clearance from the two governments in order to extend the invitation, which finally culminated in Mr. Fujita's acceptance and his appearance here today. With that, the mayor introduced Mr. Fujita who rose and approached the podium to the applause of the crowd. I looked at my children and they were all spellbound, never having seen a Japanese person before. Mr. Fujita faced the mayor and with clear and correct, but broken, English, thanked him and the people of Brookings for inviting him and making him feel so welcomed in a place where previously he had acted hostilely. He humbly apologized and asked the mayor to accept for the city a token of his gratitude and offering of peace. He unwrapped the red sheath to reveal a magnificent sword, which he held aloft with his two hands, stating it had been in his family for 400 years. The crowd erupted in applause and cheers at the generosity of this gift, which the mayor accepted graciously on behalf of the citizens of Brookings. There was much bowing after that and the mayor thanked the audience for coming and announced the subsequent festivities of the day.

People were leaving the stage area but I noticed Jack come from behind the other veterans and approach the podium, where Mr. Fujita stood with the mayor and his family. He spoke to the mayor who shook his hand and then he turned to Mr. Fujita and bowed. He said something to him, then held out his hand, which Mr. Fujita took. They held hands as they conversed for several minutes. Then Jack released his hand and saluted the man, a gesture Mr. Fujita respectfully returned. There were tears in my eyes at the momentousness of the scene: two former enemies, showing respect and honor for one another. I was proud to know this man and thrilled that my children were here to see such a historically significant moment.

"Mom, what do you think they are saying to each other?" Amy was asking me.

"I don't know, maybe they are talking about the sword or about their both being pilots. We'll have to wait and ask Jack," I responded to her.

Jack was saying goodbye to the man in the wheelchair, so we walked over to wait for him by the stairs. "Let's go get something to drink, I'm a little parched," he said as he led us away from the stage over to where the refreshments were. The way the kids were hanging on him, I could tell they were filled with pride and admiration for him. As we sat at a picnic table, Amy, ever curious, asked him, "So what were you talking about?"

Jack chuckled and said, "Nothing special, I just told him I honored him and his bravery during the war. And that just as I forgave him for his actions, I hoped he could forgive me mine, which he very kindly did."

"But what did you need to be forgiven for?" Amy asked.

Before Jack would even try to answer that question, I told Amy it was not polite to pry, for which she apologized.

"It's okay, Jenny," he said to me, then turned to Amy. "It was really just a way to make him feel less guilty. We were both fighting for our countries, doing what we were asked to do, to cause destruction. It wasn't personal. And I wanted to acknowledge that for him."

"That was really nice of you," she said as she finished her lemonade. "Mom, can I go play with those kids over there?"

I looked up to see children playing on some swings and told her it was okay. And with that, they all ran off in different directions to be with kids their own ages. Jack and I were left alone there at the table. He got up and came to my side and held my hand. "I didn't want to tell her that Mr. Fujita and I had both killed a lot of each other's countrymen."

"Amy was right. That was nice of you," I said sincerely. "How did you really feel meeting him?"

"It was a little strange, but after all this time, I no longer feel any hostility toward any Japanese. Though that wasn't always the case." He paused, staring off into the distance, as if he was trying to find the right words to say something difficult. He came back to looking at me, smiled and said, "It felt good to meet him, to be able to express my sorrow for any damage I may have caused, especially since he is so peaceful and so apologetic. And such a humble man. Not at all like my memories of the Japanese in the camps. It was good to meet a Japanese man and not feel hatred or a desire for revenge."

I felt as though there was something he wasn't saying, but didn't press him. "Can I thank you?" I asked.

He looked at me, puzzled and asked, "For what?"

"For bringing us here, for sharing this part of your life with me. . .and the kids. They learned a lot today and I could tell how much they admired you watching you on that stage."

"Well, let's just say we all learned a lot today."

We sat there awhile, watching the kids, when Tommy came running back and asked if he could go to the Harbor where there was a party going on. Jack and I looked at each other, and I said, "Sure, but let's all go."

Port Orford 1964

We had just finished Sunday breakfast; the kids had all scattered. Tommy and Jimmy ran off to play with their friends down on the beach. Mary and Amy were in their room playing the Beatles record. "She loves you, yeah, yeah, yeah. She loves you, yeah, yeah, yeah." I'd been listening to that for the last two weeks and was pretty sick of it. Mary at 13 was star-struck over this mop-headed group from England. That was all she could seem to talk about and Amy was right there with her. What a phenomenon they were. It seemed all the teenage girls across the country had lost their minds over these four.

Jack and I were enjoying the last of the coffee, chatting about our weeks. I told him about CJ cutting his finger pretty badly and having to rush over to the doctor to get stitched up and then came right back to work, slicing, dicing and grilling. Jack asked if it was the same doctor who had treated him.

"No, we have a new doctor now. Doc was in his 70's and had arthritis really bad. He decided he needed a drier climate and moved to Arizona. That was two years ago. I hear from him every Christmas. He's doing fine there. . .plays golf and volunteers at a small free clinic a couple of days a week," I explained, remembering the man so fondly.

"That's too bad. Oh, no, I'm happy he is doing well. It's just that I would have loved to thank him for treating me so well. The doctors at Oak Bluff, where I went after here, commented on how well my burns had been treated. One said I was lucky, that the treatment I received was the best method and that if I had been treated otherwise, I might have had infection or been scarred far worse than he thought I would be.

I think they were right. The three of us left here and recovered faster than many of the other burn victims that were there."

"I'll have to write and tell Doc. He was happy for me when I told him you were back in my life and that I was really happy with you. He wasn't crazy about Tom. Wasn't happy about the way my life was going with him. Wasn't happy about the way he turned out," I stopped, remembering some pretty unhappy times, especially the revelation about his finger.

"Don't be sad. That part of your life is over, except that he gave you four really great kids. And I am happy to hear that you are happy with me." He smiled and reached for my hand. "Quite honestly, the last two years have been the happiest of my life. I am crazy about you, and your kids, and every moment we spend together. It is all precious to me. And I don't want anything to change what you and I have together." He was serious and ponderous, seemed to be choosing his words carefully. "That's why I haven't asked you to marry me. I got married twice, both times I thought they were the one. Of course, I was drunk most of the time then and couldn't see anything clearly. And both times, they were the wrong women. Both ended miserably and I know it's my fault. I know that after the wedding and the honeymoon, my actions and behavior changed and they left. Or, ran, would be a better word." He paused and looked in my eyes. "I don't want to take the chance that things would change if we got married. I don't want to lose you or what we have together," he said beseechingly. "And I couldn't be any more committed to you with a marriage license."

"Jack, when it comes to choosing spouses, you don't win the prize. My choice wasn't all that good either," I said, trying to relieve some of the guilt he was feeling. "Besides, I don't want to risk anything changing between us either. As far as I am concerned, the closeness and connection that we share is all I want, all I ever wanted. We have had a marriage of our souls. You have my heart and that is all that matters."

Jack leaned over to kiss me as Jimmy came flying in the door. "Mom, Mom, come quick. Tommy is missing." He was crying and talking fast and looked more scared than I'd ever seen him look.

"Calm down, Jimmy, what do you mean missing?"

"He went out in a boat with Ricky and we can't see him anymore."

"Where did you see him last?"

"Out by the rocks. They were sailing in and around the big rocks off shore and suddenly we couldn't see him anymore."

I ran to the phone and called the Sheriff, trying to remain calm and not unleash the panic that was building inside me. He told me he was just about to call me, that a fisherman on the dock had noticed them too far out in the little sailfish they were in. The wind had just shifted and was blowing strong, so he knew they were in trouble and called it in. The Coast Guard was on their way to search for them.

"What can I do?" I cried. I looked at Jack. He was holding Jimmy, trying to soothe him and his fears.

"Go on down to the dock. I'll meet you there and we can wait for word on my radio," he said.

I dropped the phone, ran to get the girls and with Jack and Jimmy, we ran down the hill to the dock. It was cloudy and blowing pretty hard, but thankfully, there was no fog. We could see pretty far out to the horizon. Sheriff Johnson was already there, talking on his radio. We ran to him.

"They've launched the boat and the helicopter has left Coos Bay, should be out here in about 20 minutes," he said as I got next to him.

Jack was behind me and had his arms around me to keep me from shivering. He spoke to the Sheriff, "I'm a pilot and have a plane in Gold Beach, would it help if I went out to look as well?"

"No. They have a pretty good idea of where to look. And by the time you get to your plane and get back here, it'll be nearly two hours. I think they'll find them by then." The sheriff looked at Jack and the way he was holding me and the kids and added, "Besides, I think you are much better use right here."

We stood there huddled together staring out at sea, all scared out of our wits, praying that Tommy would come back to us. I remembered his birth, my first. He was the sweetest little baby, always wanting to cuddle. And such a good boy, never gave me any trouble. He'd had his share of boyhood incidents: coming home muddy and soaked after playing in a big mud puddle, breaking his arm on the jungle gym, having a near fatal crash after riding his bike down the hill, losing all track of time while playing with his friends and not coming home till after dark, with me calling all over town looking for him, numerous cuts and scraped knees, but never did anything bad. He always told the truth, tried to do the right thing with the other kids, was always loving and considerate to me. All of this was running through my brain as I stood trembling, transfixed on the sea, oblivious to everything else going on around me. Someone brought over a bench from the restaurant and Jack made us all sit down. Then I noticed Ricky's mom Pamela next to me. I threw my arms around her and we held each other for a long time, consoling each other with reassurances they would be found. . .alive. I felt a tap on my shoulder. It was Verna pushing a cup of something hot into my hands. It was then I noticed there were many people on the dock, many familiar faces, all standing around, waiting with us for news. Verna gave me a hug and kissed my forehead. "Drink," she said. I took a sip. It was warm. Coffee and . . . whiskey. It felt good going down. I thanked her, and continued drinking. It made me feel warm inside and I stopped shaking a little.

The Sheriff was on his radio and I asked Jack how long it had been. He said a little over an hour. An hour. My God. I knew how cold that water was. I sat there shivering, knowing how cold my baby was, unable to hold back my fears and the river of tears pouring down my face, holding on for dear life to Pamela's hand.

"They've found them," the Sheriff yelled. "They've spotted them hanging on to their boat. It's flipped over and they're holding onto each other's hands." A big hoot went up from the crowd, I jumped up and grabbed onto my kids with Jack's arms around all of us. We were all crying and thanking God. The Sheriff had the radio on and we heard "Divers in the water," from the other end. I took hold of Jimmy who was truly suffering—crying more than me—and told him it was going to be alright. . . Tommy was found. I knew he felt guilty for not stopping Tommy. It was Ricky's boat and Tommy knew nothing about sailing, but they were all having so much fun, he didn't stop him. He kept saying he was sorry. I held him tight and told him it was alright, there was no way he could have known this would happen, that they were just being boys having an adventure. I was telling this to Jimmy but it was really *me* that I was trying to calm into not feeling guilty.

We could see the helicopter off in the distance hovering over the water. It seemed like hours but was really only minutes before we saw it moving closer to us—they were finally coming in. I noticed the sheriff was sitting in his car with the door closed on the radio and suddenly I was filled with dread.

They were found, but were they alive? I couldn't bear the not knowing, but just kept saying to myself, "He's okay, he's okay." My heart was aching and my stomach churning, the seconds ticking endlessly by. Finally, the helicopter was near the end of the dock, getting ready to set down. The wind from the rotor was blowing up all sorts of debris, like a tornado, making it impossible to keep my eyes open. At long last, I heard the engine stop and felt the wind diminish. Eventually the rotor stopped and we ran toward the open door. There was Tommy, huddled in a blanket, his eyes closed. "Is he alright?" I screamed. The diver looked at me and with a smile, said, "He's cold, Ma'am, but he's alive." He started to hand Tommy down to Jack. "You need to get him warm. You might want to get him to the hospital, have him checked. But by all means, get him warm."

Jack was racing with Tommy, back to the Sheriff's car, which was running with the heat on. I looked to the diver to see about Ricky. Pamela was next to me, asking for her son. The diver asked if she was his mother and she said yes, Ricky was her boy. The diver jumped down to the dock and stood in front of her, and told her he was sorry, but that her boy was dead. I felt the air get sucked out of me and grabbed hold of her, as she screamed, "Noooooooo." She was collapsing, and I tried to hold her up. The Sheriff grabbed hold of her to keep her from falling to the ground. She was crying hysterically and calling her boy's name. My heart broke for her and I wanted to stay with her, but I knew I had to get to Tommy, that precious time was passing. Jimmy was beside me tugging my sleeve, telling me we had to go, we had to get Tommy to the doctor, so I handed Pamela off to another woman standing there who was her friend. I ran with Jimmy to the car. Jack got out of the car and handed Tommy off to me. I clamped my arms tightly around him and kissed him over and over, feeling the cold from his body seeping into me. I was about to say "let's go" to get to the doctor's office, when the door opened and the doctor climbed in the back seat with us. He had come to us and was holding Tommy's forehead, which I knew was ice cold. He said, "Let's go to my office where my equipment is." The deputy jumped in the car and said he'd drive us. Jack told me to go, he would take the kids home and take care of them. With that, we were off.

At his office, the doctor rushed Tommy inside and put him on an exam table. He turned on the heat in the room, then unpeeled the blanket and cut off his wet clothes. He listened to his breathing, took his pulse, blood pressure and his temperature, then rewrapped him in the blanket. "He doesn't seem to be in distress, all his vitals are in the normal range, except for his temperature, which is 94. We've just got to get him warmed up, but not too quickly. We'll just keep him warm here and I'll keep checking him." Then, he added, "If you need to take care of your other kids, I can watch over Tommy."

"Oh, no, I don't want to leave him. Besides, someone is watching my kids. But I would like to call them, if I can use your phone."

"Of course," he said and led the way into his office, showed me the phone and left to get back to Tommy.

Jack picked up the phone right away and I told him Tommy was going to be okay, which he repeated to the kids hovering around him. I heard them cheer. Then I asked him if he could stay. Without a moment's hesitation, he responded, "Jen, don't worry about anything here. I am here as long as you need me to be. And by the way, CJ called and said you have the week off, that he got someone to cover for you. So, if it's okay with you, I'd like to stay the week."

"Of course, it's okay. It's more than okay, really. It's going to be a tough week and I will be thrilled to have you here.

Tommy will, too." I asked about Jimmy and he told me he had settled down and seemed okay. Holding back the flood of emotions pouring over me, I told him, "I'm going to stay here until his temperature rises and he regains consciousness. I don't know how long that will be, but I'll call you when the doctor says I can take him home."

"Okay, but don't worry about anything here."

"I won't. And Jack? Thank you for being here for me, for us." I managed to get out before the tears started to fall.

"You don't have to thank me, Jen. Though I wish the circumstances were better, I am very happy to be here. Now go be with Tommy and we'll see you soon."

I went back into the exam room and the doctor suggested I lay next to Tommy and hold him, explaining that my body heat would help him to warm up. So, I did. I climbed onto the table behind Tommy, wrapped my arms around him and began to rock him, humming a lullaby into his head, as I did when he was a baby.

*

I wasn't wrong when I said it would be a tough week; this was the worst week in my life that I could remember. Other bad things had happened in my life, like when Pa died, or when Tom died, but then it was over and life slowly went back to normal. This was different. My first-born son, who was like an extension of myself, was getting over a traumatic, near-death experience, the aftereffects of hypothermia and deep-seated guilt over the death of his friend, which was prolonged by a full-blown Catholic funeral. My heart broke for him, and for Pamela, who was so gracious. Although Jack and I repeatedly told Tommy he wasn't responsible for Ricky's death, Pamela saying it made him believe it, or perhaps accept is a better word. I hung back, as they clung to each other throughout the service and at the cemetery and let them cry together, mourn together—seeming to gain strength and fortitude from one another.

It looked like the whole town showed up at the funeral, everyone in shock and feeling the weight of a child being lost so tragically. It was the first time in my lifetime that that had happened in this town. Yes, children had died from illness, but never from a fluke accident. But it reminded us once again of the dangers of the sea, how what starts out as a beautiful, calm day can rapidly deteriorate into a life-threatening tempest. Tommy had told me that Ricky was fearless, he always wanted to push his environment and his situation to the extreme. It was Ricky who wanted to go out past the rocks, where the wind was stronger, to see how fast their little boat could go. Tommy tried to dissuade him, but he told Tommy not to worry, he'd done it before and it was really fun, so they went. When they got out past the safety of the headland, the wind shifted and intensified. Their sail was ripped off before they could even put it down. They were powerless and were pushed further out to sea, where the waves were bigger. Before they could even think about how to get back, the boat was flipped over and they were in the sea. They managed to get back to the hull and held each other's hands across the beam, until someone would come along and rescue them. But the water was so cold, they were shivering and soon Ricky became unresponsive. Tommy just kept holding onto his wrists, so he wouldn't slide off. Soon, he felt himself slipping into unconsciousness and lashed a rope still attached to the boat around their wrists, in case he passed out too. He told me he thought about me, about how mad I was going to be at him and that was the last thing he remembered until he woke up in my arms on the doctor's exam table, crying and saying he was sorry, over and over again. I held him tight and through my own tears told him I forgave him, I wasn't mad at him, that I was so glad he was okay. After a few moments of euphoria, he asked me how Ricky was and I had to tell him the sad news. I watched him dissemble into a pit of deep sorrow and guilt, where he had stayed all week. Now, I was wondering if he would ever come out of it.

It had been two days since the burial and he was still moping around, not wanting to go anywhere or do anything. He mostly stayed in his room, just lying on his bed, being morose. Jack tried especially hard to draw him out, to get him to talk about what he was feeling, thinking he might be more willing to talk about it with a man, but nothing seemed to work. Jimmy, Mary and Amy went back to their routines after a few days, but still there was a cloud over their behavior—they were not quite as gay as they had been prior to the incident. Jack and I were not exempt. We spent our days trying to lighten spirits and fell exhausted into bed at night. I spent a fair amount of time beating myself up, feeling it was my fault this had happened, that I'd been too lenient—giving the children too much freedom—that I should have kept them on shorter leashes. I went to visit Pamela to see how she was doing and we spent several hours talking about our feelings, and we commiserated. She was feeling just the same as I, laden with guilt. Last night, at the dinner table when the meal was finished and before everyone scattered, I told my kids how I felt, wanting to give them a chance to share what they were feeling. They sat quietly and listened to every word.

"Look, when I was growing up here, my parents gave me the same kind of freedom that I have always given you. There were a few rules, like, don't get in a stranger's car, don't leave town without telling one of them, be home for supper and before dark. Those are the rules I gave to you. I never wanted to stop you from exploring or having new experiences. I felt that in this small town, someone would see what you were doing or know where you were. I never wanted to stop you from having a childhood. . .a healthy childhood where you would learn your own lessons."

Amy, who was so much wiser then her eleven years of age, said, "Mom, you always taught us right from wrong. And being able to decide what was okay to do made me smarter and stronger. I have always been so happy to have a Mom who gave me that freedom. Mary Lou has to ask her Mom before she does everything and her Mom is always telling her 'No, don't do that.' So, I, for one, am very glad you are the way you are."

I was so proud of that little girl, I wanted to cry. Mary chimed in, "Yeah, Mom, you can't blame yourself for a freak of nature. If the wind hadn't shifted, they would have sailed back to the beach and we wouldn't have even known he was out there."

"Except for me, I knew he was out there," Jimmy said a bit angrily, "And I did nothing to stop him." He was crying again.

"Jimmy, look, I told you there was no way you could have known about the wind or that the fun would turn dangerous," I tried again to dissolve his guilt.

"Stop it," Tommy yelled. He was furious. "This is nobody's fault but mine. Not yours, Jimmy, not yours, Mom. I got Ricky killed. I should have known better than to go so far out. But I was too bent on having fun and feeling the speed and the wind in my face, I didn't stop to think of what could happen. I threw all caution to the wind and just went for it. I wish I had died on that boat, like Ricky. I wish I was dead," and with that, he dissolved in tears. I started to run to him, but Jack stopped me, told me to let him be.

We all just sat there too numb to move, watching him suffer, crying so hard he was shaking.

After a minute or so, Jack said, "Tommy. I am not your father, but I couldn't love you more if I were. Mary is right. What happened out there was a fluke of nature. The best seaman in a bigger boat could have found himself in the same situation. So, this is not your fault. Instead of beating yourself up, why not channel that energy into something positive. Raise some money and build a memorial for Ricky or buy some books for the library in his name, or give it to his mom for a college fund for his sister, whatever you think Ricky would want you to do. Just don't sit here feeling guilty and sorry for yourself. None of you. And Jenny, don't change the rules in this house. The freedom you have given these kids has made them into the fine, respectful and respectable people they are. I have so much admiration for you and what you have done for your family, for the values you have instilled in them and the rights you have given them to become the strong, independent individuals you

148

all are." He stopped speaking and I noticed there were watery eyes all around the table. Amy jumped up and gave Jack a big hug and a kiss on the cheek. "Would it be alright if I called you Dad?" she asked. Jimmy and Mary got up and joined them in a big family hug. Tommy seemed to rise up from the depths of his sorrow, wiped the tears from his eyes, went to Jack and asked, "Me too?" and the mood in the room changed instantly to one of joy. "I'd like that," Jack said and from then on, he was Dad.

Port Orford 1965

"Oregon Marine Dies in Combat," was today's headline. Sadly, more and more young men were being called into service, sent to Southeast Asia, and dying there. I wasn't the only one who was angry about it. College students and religious groups across the country were banding together to protest. The nightly news and newspapers were filled with horrible images of combat. It was all very up-close and personal. The slow and antiquated media that existed during prior wars was gone; we were seeing the carnage in real time, practically live, and it was brutal. The thought that my son and his friends would be 18 in two more years was agonizing. I prayed this awful war would end before that.

As much as it was bothering me, it was bothering Jack even more. He was being forced to remember his own experiences and to relive it, in his dreams, or should I say, nightmares. More than once I woke to his thrashing about and yelling something in Japanese. He was back in the camp, suffering some brutality, being tortured. When he woke out of it, he never wanted to talk about the dream, just held onto me and said something like, "I'm alright as long as you hold me."

But last night was different. When he woke, he was crying and shaking. I held him and soothed him and asked him to tell me about the dream. He was reluctant, but I insisted. "Jack, the only way to stop these dreams is to talk about them, unleash them from your subconscious."

He sat there for a few minutes, shaking off the reality of the dream and trying to compose himself. "I had made a friend in camp. Louis. He was just a kid. A Marine from Arkansas. He was thin to begin with and after months in the camp, he was practically skin and bones, a skeleton. We all were, but he was sick. He'd been in combat on one of the South Sea islands and had malaria and dysentery really bad. I tried to help him with the work whenever I could because he was so weak. One morning at roll call, the Camp Commander, who was a sadistic barbarian, called him out of line, told him to carry a basket of digging tools into the mine. Those baskets were heavy. Two of us healthier guys would usually carry a basket between us and struggle doing it. I knew there was no way he could carry it and so did the Commander. But Louis wouldn't give him the satisfaction of protesting or giving in, so he started walking with it. Very slowly. It was such an effort for him to take a step. We were all watching him, silently rooting for him, praying he could make it. We couldn't help him. If we tried to help him, we would be beaten or put in the hole, or both. He'd only taken a few steps, when he fell to one knee. I reacted, I wanted to run over and help him, but caught myself before I took one step. But the Commander saw me flinch and he pulled me out of line and started screaming at me inches from my face, a torrent of Japanese words I didn't understand. I could feel his spit on my face as he yelled at me for what seemed an eternity. Then he called two guards over and told them to punish me, which I understood. One stood in front of me and with all his force, hit me in the side with the butt of his rifle. I fell to the ground holding my ribs, which I felt snap. They started to kick me all over. In the chest, in the back, in the head, over and over again. The Commander yelled something and they stopped. Every part of my body hurt. I was bleeding from my head. Blood was running into my eye. He was yelling at me again. I didn't understand what he was saying, so I just lay there. Then the two guards yanked me up onto my feet. I was wobbling, trying with all my might to stay upright. He yelled for me to stand at attention, which I understood. I tried to straighten up and lift

151

my hand to my forehead. It took all my strength. He was yelling at me again, but I didn't understand. I was wavering, but held my hand in place and looked straight at him while he continued to yell at me over and over. Finally, one of the guards who spoke a little English, told me to go help my friend carry all the baskets to the mine. I saluted the Commander and said *Hai*, which means 'Yes, sir,' and turned to walk toward Louis, who was sitting on the ground with tears streaming down his face. It hurt to walk, to breathe, even to think, but I did it. I walked over to where Louis was, helped him up and together we managed to lift the basket and walk, although very slowly, to the mine. Neither one of us would give the Commander the satisfaction of showing defeat. Even beaten and sick, in our minds we were stronger than them and wanted to show it. It took us several hours, but we carried all the tools to the mine. Once inside the shaft, past the guards, the other prisoners made us lie down and did our work for us to meet the quota for the day."

I threw my arms around him and held him, shocked, sickened, deeply moved by his need to help a friend despite the personal threat to himself. "What happened to Louis?" I asked reluctantly, knowing that truth might be more than either of us could bear.

"That night, when we came out of the mine, we went to see the Medic. There wasn't much he could do for us—he had no medicine or supplies. He felt around my ribs and told me two of my ribs seemed cracked. He took some torn up shirts and tied my ribs as best he could and put both of us in the makeshift hospital so we would not have to work for a few days at least. When I woke in the morning, he told me Louis had died overnight. He was just too sick to go on anymore. I didn't feel sad for him. I was happy for him. He was free. No one would torture him again." He paused and I found myself at a loss for words, tears welling in my eyes. What could I say? I was sad for Louis and for Jack for having gone through such an ordeal. "Funny thing was, the next day, the guards stopped torturing us or making us work. We were given more food, better food, not just rice, but fish as well. We weren't sure why, but soon a rumor circulated through camp that the war was over. That the U.S. had dropped some big bomb on Japan and they had surrendered. If Louis could have held on another day, he might have made it. That's all I could think about and I started to cry for him and I couldn't stop.

"The next day, our planes flew over the camp and dropped several palettes of food, fresh water, clothing, medical supplies and newspapers. That's how we learned about how the war came to an end. There were also leaflets instructing us to sit tight, that we would be liberated. For the next two weeks, we ate plenty of k-rations, had lots of fresh water to drink and the medics were able to treat many of the sicknesses we prisoners had. Then one day, a convoy of troop carriers pulled into camp, we loaded on and left that hellish place forever. It's been years since I had a dream like that, being back in that camp, but lately, seeing what's going on in Vietnam, the memories have been coming back to me.

"And I know I am one of the lucky ones. I met guys in the camp who in the end were prisoners for over three years. It was only their will that allowed them to survive, because they were beaten and starved like thousands of others who perished, like Louis. They told stories of atrocities they had witnessed, of men who were shot for falling down from sheer exhaustion, or were bayonetted for going too slow, and men who were beheaded for not following orders they didn't even understand."

He stopped talking and I searched for something to say that would console him, make him feel less despondent, less guilty about surviving. There really was nothing I could say to make him feel better. But maybe I could help him to understand it. "Jack, when the war ended, we had hundreds of men come through our hospital from the various camps. I saw firsthand what the Japanese had done to our men. They were skinny and sick, really sick. And they had scars all over from where they'd been beaten with bamboo and rifles. They told stories just like yours and the ones you heard from others. I was appalled and horrified to think any race of people could be so brutal and barbaric. I needed to understand it. Much was written about the POW's afterwards and I read everything I could get my hands on. I read about the Japanese warrior code, I think it's called *bushido,* which instills in them a warrior attitude. As soldiers, they have rules for how to live and that death is a duty. They value honor over life, preferring to kill themselves—commit hara-kiri—than allow themselves to be captured. They believe that if you are foolish enough to be taken prisoner, then you deserve to die. It is that code that so many of the Japanese guards and commanders of the camps invoked to avoid prosecution after the war. I know that can never justify what was done to you or what you witnessed, but knowing about that difference in cultures, can maybe help you to understand your experience."

"I do understand it and I do know that so many others suffered way more than I did. My brain knows that. But some other part of me, can't seem to shake it."

"I know there are support groups for survivors of the camps. Talking about your experience might help to shake it loose. Have you ever sought one out?"

"No, it's never been an issue until recently, I think I'm just going to stop watching the news."

"I'd be happy to help you find a group. You know, I am happy to listen to you night and day, but I think talking with other men, men who have been through what you have, would be far more helpful. I think it might really help you."

He turned to put his arms around me and kissed me on the forehead. "You're all I need to be saved from the hold that camp has on me." He pulled me down into the bed, holding on to me and promised he would look into it when he got back to LA.

It was the middle of the week and pretty slow. Just the regulars, no tourists today. I was chatting with Ned at the end of the counter, when a nicely dressed man walked in and sat at the other end. I grabbed a mug and the coffee pot and headed down there. I greeted him and asked if he wanted coffee. Sure, he said. He was staring at me and finally said, "Jenny?" as a question. I looked at his face and he was somewhat familiar, though I couldn't quite place him. I continued to look at him as I poured his coffee. "I'm sorry, do we know each other?" I asked.

"I'm not surprised you don't remember me. It's only been about 20 years," he said with a laugh.

Twenty years, must be a soldier who came through the hospital. Twice before, men had come in here and knew me right away. Guess I haven't changed much in 20 years. He did look familiar, but I didn't recall him. But then, any man I had encountered in that hospital was bound to look different today. . .a few more pounds, more hair, healthier looking. It was then I noticed his left arm was missing. His sports jacket had been tailored to eliminate the sleeve. He was just about to say something, when I remembered. "Sam Gunderson," I said in amazement. "Well you do look quite a bit different from the last time I saw you. You look fabulous, as a matter of fact." He was the picture of health and affluence. Well-groomed and well-dressed, he appeared to have done well after the war. I heard my call to pick up food, handed him a menu and said, "Take a look and I'll be right back for your order," and went to get and deliver Ned's food, all the while thinking about how great Sam looked. So many of the vets who lost limbs never quite adjusted to a new way of living. Their physical limitations and their feelings of being less-than-whole made it hard to work, hard to feel successful and hard to have a good relationship with a woman. They struggled because they were unable to overcome their feelings of inadequacy and to adapt.

I went back to Sam, took his order, put it in the queue and went back to him. "You really do look wonderful, Sam. You look like you've done well for yourself," I remarked.

"I have. When I was finally discharged after many months of rehab, I couldn't imagine what I was ever going to be able to do to make a living. I was fortunate, though. My parents knew I had a head for business and gave me ten acres of land they owned outside of LA, with the understanding that I would put my brothers to work. I have two brothers, both younger than me. They were just bumming around after high school, working as carpenters or whatever they could find. So, I got a loan through the VA and started a construction company. We subdivided the land and started putting up little starter houses and before we could even finish one, it was sold. And with the profits from those houses, we bought more land and did the same thing, over and over again. Now, my brothers run the construction company and I am a developer."

I excused myself once again and went to get his order and take care of my other customers. When I got back to him I asked, "What on earth has brought you to Port Orford?"

"Well, I'm here to meet with your City Council about an idea I have for a first-class hotel and restaurant—a small resort. I've been looking the Oregon coast over and there's nothing like that for hundreds of miles. I have some sketches and a plan that I want to pitch to them. I think it could be just what this town needs to grow."

I didn't say anything to dissuade him or diminish his optimism, but I knew the Council's attitude toward new ideas. Everyone here in town knew their idea of growth, was <u>no</u> growth. There was a new couple at the counter so I had to leave him again. I had just finished getting them settled in when more people walked in the door. I went back to Sam and told him it was getting too busy for me to continue talking. I asked him to come back at 2 when I was done for the day and we could have lunch together, which he agreed to do. I gave him his check and ran off to waiting, hungry customers.

Before I knew it, I was cleaning up the counter and my work station, when Sam walked back in the door. I walked over to him, welcomed him back and led him to the booth at the far end of the room. Verna came over as soon as we sat down and I introduced her to Sam. I ordered my usual, tuna salad on rye with a ginger ale, which Sam said sounded good. Verna brought us some water and left us to catch up.

Sam asked what I'd been doing since we saw each other last and I told him my story in a nutshell, about marriage, having children, becoming a widow and coming to work here at CJ's. I was just finishing telling my story when Verna arrived with our food. We got settled in and started to eat. I asked Sam to tell me about where he went immediately after Portland and what his therapy was like. He proceeded to tell me that, just like Jack, he was taken to Oak Bluff, where there was a huge prosthetic and rehabilitation center. Since his arm was completely gone, a prosthetic was not an option for him, so he basically had occupational therapy. They taught him how to do things with just one arm and hand. Fortunately, he had been right-handed which is the arm he still had, so having to learn to write wasn't necessary. They showed him tips for grooming and dressing himself with one arm. He said the only thing he really couldn't do was tie his shoes, but fortunately they made slip-on shoes. After three months, they discharged him and sent him home. He was grateful for the support of his family, including the land donation from his parents, for without that, he might have lived his life on disability.

'It doesn't sound like the loss of an arm has held you back at all," I remarked.

"No, it hasn't really. I met a wonderful girl, got married and we have two great kids. . .girls, ages eight and ten. But I'd be lying if I didn't say that I wished sometimes to be able to hold my wife with two arms or to hold both my daughters' hands, but those moments are rare. I try always to live my life to the fullest and not allow myself to be held back from doing anything. I drive a car, I surf, I ski. I have no complaints."

"That's wonderful. I'm happy for you. Glad to hear you have daughters. I'm worried sick my sons are going to have to go to Vietnam. My oldest will be 18 next year and graduating, and Jimmy is one year behind him. Unless this thing winds down suddenly, they're going to have to go."

"I feel for you, I really do. This war isn't like our war. And I think the government is lying to us about it. They say we're making progress, winning, but the press reports don't seem to back that up."

"I know. Every night on the news, it just gets more and more awful and it's like the war is taking place right in our living room. You've been in combat, you know what war is like firsthand, but for me, the images are so graphic and bloody, and just plain horrifying. Day after day, young men are being killed and wounded and I do not want my boys there, but I'm powerless to stop it."

"More and more people are feeling disillusioned. Young men are wondering why they should put their lives on the line for a little country in Southeast Asia. They're not buying into the whole "save democracy" idea. That's why many are fleeing to Canada, where the government can't touch them."

"Is that my son's only option? He'd be out of my life and be imprisoned if he came back here. I don't want him to be a criminal."

"Well then, you wouldn't want him to join the Resistance. There are other options that are not criminal, like being a conscientious objector. If he were a member of a peace-church, like the Amish, or the Mennonites, he could avoid serving. Or if he were enrolled in a seminary. Or a homosexual, the Army won't take homosexuals. Oh, I know, have him join the Coast Guard. Although it's harder to get in there, he wouldn't have to face combat, even though he might get sent over there. They're there to patrol the coastline, secure the ports and board and inspect local boats for arms and ammunition. They have had very few casualties. If I had a son, I think that is what I would advise him to do."

"Thank you for all that information. You know so much more about it than I do," I remarked and then suddenly my mind went in a different direction. I thought of Jack and his nightmares. "I told you earlier about Jack coming back into my life. Well, he was in the Pacific arena, like you. He was a Navy pilot and got shot down and taken prisoner by the Japanese. He was in a camp in Japan for about 15 months and like every prisoner of war, he was starved, beaten, brutalized in many ways, and lately has been having terrible nightmares. He is truly tortured. I suggested to him to find a veterans group, men who were prisoners like him. I thought it might help if he could talk to other men who are probably experiencing similar debilitating dreams. By any chance, are you part of or do you know of a group like that in southern California? He lives and works in LA."

"I don't know of any group, but I do know some POW's. I've given a couple of them jobs, because they can't seem to keep it together on a consistent, long-term basis. Alcohol is a common form of treatment for them.   But I keep them on because I know most employers won't stand for it. I just tell them no drinking on the job and if they can't come to work for any reason, they have to call me. That's it, just two rules. And they're grateful. We treat them with respect and they stay sober enough to make it to work. I could arrange a get-together with Jack if you think that would help."

"Jack had his own battle with alcohol, but has been sober for years. He's managed to create a very successful business, like you, but these nightmares are tearing him up and they seem to be more frequent. That's why I think talking about them and his experiences with someone who's been through the same thing would help him to get beyond the trauma."

"Sure, I'd be happy to give him a call and meet him when I get back. Now, what do you think of my idea for a fine hotel and restaurant overlooking the harbor?"

"I thought Californians think of this state as having nothing to offer, other than trees and rain," I said jokingly. "Do you really believe they would want to come all the way here, when there are so many wonderful hotels and restaurants right in their own state?"

"I do. But it's not just Californians. People from all over the west and especially the south, would love to come here for a respite from their hot and dry environments. The I-5 is about to be completed between Washington and California, making this entire state accessible to visitors. And I've already met with the folks at the airport in Gold Beach. They're able to accept charter flights from San Francisco, Los Angeles or Portland which would open up this place to the whole country. And what really got me thinking about this idea was my sense that attitudes about this state are changing. I was running into people who had been here and were talking about it, in a good way. California is getting more and more crowded and people are longing for open spaces and clean air and this place certainly has that to offer. And what I plan to build here is something unique, something representative of the heritage and history of the state."

"Well, it sounds like you've done your research. I wish you luck with the Council." Verna came to the table to remove our dishes and announce they were closing for the day. Sam offered to pay for lunch, but I told him it was on the house, one of my free lunches that I was allowed. He thanked me and Verna, and tried to leave her a tip, which she also declined. "See, I know I am right about this town. Great service and friendly people," he remarked as we walked out the door. Outside, I thanked him for all his helpful information and gave him Jack's business phone number. I told him to let me know how it went with the council, gave him a hug and a wave as he walked on down to his motel.

＊

Jack and I had our spot on the parade route right outside the movie theater. It was really the only spot on the whole route where you could get a great view and be in the shade, to avoid getting fried in the sun. We could see and hear the vehicles about ten blocks away, crawling down the main street. The annual 4th of July parade was quite a crowd pleaser. Both sides of the street were lined with people—the whole town had come to see the show.

"You could have ridden on the Veteran's float," I said to Jack as I snuggled up to him. "I wouldn't have minded seeing you in uniform again," remembering how handsome he looked in his dress blues.

"No. I confess I am not feeling very patriotic these days. Maybe some other year, but now, I'm not at all happy with what our government is doing with this damned war."

I nodded in agreement. It seemed every day there was a newscast about a new massacre of civilians. Whole villages were being shot or burned down, mostly by the North Vietnamese and the Viet Cong. So many innocent people were being murdered, not just as collateral damage, but outright slaughters. The anti-war protests were growing more prevalent, with larger groups of people marching. Every city, every town, even this one had signs of protest displayed. Looking around here, I saw quite a few "Stop the War" signs, shirts and caps, and lots of peace signs. The media was intent on bringing the truth to the world, showing images of our own soldiers looking bedraggled and defeated, so many wounded, with dirty looking bandages. They didn't want to be there, and it showed. This was not a defensible war and it continued to drag on, to weigh on the country. Month after month, with more and more troops being sent, several from right here in Port Orford, more of them were dying, being maimed. What were we fighting for anyway?

I was snapped back to reality by the loud honk of the fire engine's horn. The parade was upon us and I was looking for my kids. They were all in it, or at least three of them were. They'd been preparing for it for weeks, working on their floats and costumes. All very secret, too. Just then the Veteran's float passed in front of us; we saluted them as they waved to the crowd. There was one old gentleman in a wheel chair—he was the only living veteran of WWI in our town—plus there were six or seven men from WWII and three younger men from the Korean War. A few were wearing their uniforms, but most were in street clothes, just wearing a cap that signified they were military.

Right behind them was the Miss America float, five young ladies on a float decorated like the American flag and there was my Mary all decked out in red, white and blue, smiling and waving just like a beauty queen. Each of the girls wore a white sundress decorated with red and blue sequins. She'd curled her hair and wore a glittering tiara, with red lipstick and a ribbon across her body that said "Miss America." She was growing to be a beautiful young lady, tall and curvy in all the right places. It seemed overnight she lost interest in the Beatles and was now far more interested in boys. And, of course, they were interested in her, creating new challenges. She was a girly girl, but remained an A student, with good values, the perfect little beauty queen. We waved back, so proud of her, as she passed in front of us.

There were lots of sheep and horses parading before us from the 4H club, then a few floats from local businesses. Next, came a float that looked like a space capsule, all covered in silver foil, and there was Jimmy, my little astronaut. He had been totally consumed by the space program, following all the NASA space launches and the most recent space docking. He told us he wanted to join the program and be an astronaut when he grew up, which didn't surprise me. He'd always loved science—it was his favorite subject. He'd won quite a few Science Project awards in school. I was impressed by the float he had worked on with a few other boys, and the creativeness of his costume. Completely dressed in white, carrying a white motorcycle helmet under his arm and the letters "NASA" across his chest, he too was waving and beaming with pride. I was filled with love for him and was waving like crazy until he spotted me. I threw him a kiss to let him know how proud I was of him.

Next came a collection of old cars which had been restored and decorated for the holiday. The Mayor was in one of the cars and next was the Grand Marshall in a convertible, Hedy Clark, who was about 95 years old and had been in this town her whole life. She lived up the Elk River in a converted old barn and still had an outhouse, not uncommon in the more rural areas. Next, was a big log truck loaded with a few colossal, cut trees, followed by a few more local floats: The Garden Club, which was beautifully decorated with flowers, the Rotary Club, the Knights of Columbus.

Behind them was a tractor being driven by my son Tommy, who had told me he was too old to be in a parade and had been acting very mysterious all week. And now I knew why. He'd been talked into towing a float. It said "Beaches belong to the People" and "Protect our Birthright." Painted tan with red and purple starfishes, and blue at the bottom depicting the ocean, there stood my daughter waving a sign that said, "Support House Bill 1601" on one side and, "Write your

Legislator" on the other. As always, she was wearing a shirt with a big peace symbol painted on it. My eyes filled with tears, I was so darn proud of her. I squeezed Jack's arm and he squeezed me back. I think I saw a tear in his eye too. She was my little fighter, my activist daughter. Always rooting for the underdog, always wanting to fight for what was right. She managed to align herself with all sorts of causes that she felt passionately about. She'd sell lemonade to make money to send to charities like "Save the Whales." Or place a hand-painted sign on a trash can that said, "Please don't litter." Of late, she was enamored with our newly elected governor, Tom McCall, a real champion for the state. Any cause he was for, she was right behind him. Presently, saving the beaches for the public and not the private domain became her latest cause célèbre, ever since she saw that photo of the Governor confronting a motel owner who was trying to block off the beach to anyone other than his motel guests. Thanks to her efforts and those of thousands like her, that bill would ultimately pass, making all coastal beaches in the entire state a birthright of the people. She was waving and when she saw me beaming at her, broke into a big smile. She knew I was proud of her and she was getting lots of cheers from the crowd. Everyone in town knew she was self-less and passionate and always had a message. They liked her message today.

She was very close to the end of the parade—all I could see remaining were a bunch of old tractors—so when she passed from my sight, I told Jack I wanted to leave. Anxious to get to the starting point where they were all headed, I couldn't wait to see my kids. I was so filled with pride for their hard work, their creativeness and their enthusiasm and I wanted to tell them. I gave them each a big hug and told them how proud I was, except for Tommy. When I saw him, I said, "Too old for a parade, huh?"

"You know how she is, Mom, she wouldn't let up till I said yes."

"I was proud to see you out there supporting your sister. You're a good big brother," I told him as I gave him a hug.

"Okay," I said, "who's hungry?"

They were all hungry, but Amy said they had to return the tractor and the trailer on which she'd made her float to the farmer just outside of town. So off we all went to make the return before heading down to the beach for a great 4th of July lunch.

*

"By the way, I met your friend Sam last week. He's a really nice guy. Couldn't stop going on and on about you, said you'd saved him," Jack said with a big smile, "which I didn't find hard to believe."

I smiled too at the memory of when we first met. "Yeah, he is a great guy. And I really didn't do anything to save him, the doctors did that. All I did was change his bandages and give him sponge baths."

"Well, they must have been great sponge baths because you certainly made an impression. He seems to think you did a lot more than that for him and I have no doubt your kindness made all the difference to him. Oh, he told me to tell you, the Council shot him down. Said they were polite and listened to everything he had to say and looked at his drawings like they were really interested, but the vote was 4 to 1 against."

"I sort of figured that would happen, but I didn't want to burst his bubble. They're really against development here, especially by Californians. Did he say what he's going to do now?"

"He's going to pitch it to Bandon, thinks they might be more receptive. He's going to add in a golf course to the resort, says the game is becoming more and more popular."

"Good for him. He might be right about the receptivity up there. They do a great deal to promote tourism. But tell me about your meeting with Sam. Did he tell you about his friends who were prisoners of war?"

"More than that. They were there at his house, which is really nice, by the way. I got to meet his wife and girls. Lovely family. But they left us and we men sat there and talked. These guys were at different camps, but we shared a lot of the same experiences, though after talking to them, I feel like I was on a vacation. They're still suffering the effects, far worse than I. They both drink, but they are doing better, thanks to your friend. If it wasn't for Sam, they would be on the street."

"Did you tell them about your nightmares?" I ventured to ask, not sure if it was too personal.

"Yeah, I talked about it and so did they. We shared stories and I have to say that I really felt better when I left, because these guys had it so much worse than I did. They both were prisoners since early in 1942, over three years. One of them, Fred, after about six months as a prisoner was taken out of a camp in the West Indies and sent to Burma as slave labor to build a railroad. The stories he told were incomprehensible. There were only a few thousand men—Australians, British, Dutch and Americans—and they built 250 miles of railroad with countless bridges with their bare hands. They had no tools, no machinery and lived under the most horrific conditions in a tropical jungle. Barely any food, no medicines for horrible diseases. He saw so many men die horrible deaths. Some of the things he described I couldn't even wrap my head around. The other guy survived the Bataan Death March and over three years in camps in the Philippines. His memories were worse than Fred's, which is hard to imagine.

"I must say, talking about some of the things we saw, things we did, things that were done to us actually felt cathartic. It was good. We're going to get together again next month. Maybe if we keep talking, we can all get rid of our demons."

"That's wonderful," I said as I scanned the beach to make sure my kids were all in sight. They were, all with their friends, being kids, having fun. "Can I talk to you about something else?"

"Sure, you can talk to me about anything."

"It's about Tommy. You know, next year, he'll graduate and have to register for the draft. I don't know if Sam mentioned it to you, but he and I talked about it and he told me several different ways that Tommy can avoid being drafted." I went on to tell him all the options that Sam told me were available to avoid going to Vietnam or at least into combat. I wanted his opinion and his support when I talked to Tommy, which I knew I needed to do soon. He was about to start his last year of school and would need to start moving in the direction of the chosen option to have a credible excuse for deferment. We agreed that we didn't want him to do anything criminal, that would brand him for life, so leaving the country and refusing to register were out. That only left religion or homosexuality as ways to avoid the draft altogether, and knowing Tommy, I didn't think he would go for either one of those. . .which left the Coast Guard. He might be lucky enough to get stationed somewhere else but if he did get sent to Vietnam, he would be safer out in the water than in combat on land.

Jack was in complete agreement with my conclusions and as we talked, we decided to let the conversation wait until after Labor Day, to allow Tommy to enjoy his last summer of fun. I laid back against Jack's chest and we sat there together mesmerized by the waves and the clouds in the warmth of the sun. . .feeling safe and at peace, despite the fact that the rest of the country was in turmoil. I thanked God every day that we lived someplace so isolated. We were immune to the race riots and civil rights' marches that were turning so violent, the outward hostilities of the KKK, and black activists being shot or hanged—horrible acts that were so foreign to us here in this small town on the very edge of the country. We were so far removed from the protests of Americans against the war, some of which turned violent when the police tried to stop them. We were in a time of great upheaval; the status quo was no longer accepted. How times had changed since World War II. Even though Sam gave up an arm, Jack was tortured, and with so many dead or missing, our country was united. People of all races were willing to do whatever was necessary, sacrifice anything and everything for the war effort, do whatever their government asked them to do, we were all Americans. But now, we were being torn apart, whites against blacks, and a government that its citizens felt couldn't be trusted, that they believed had lied to its people. The cry of a seagull brought me back to the present and I tried hard to block these thoughts from my mind and just enjoy being in the arms of a man I loved in the safety of a harmonious community by the sea.

*

Sitting on my couch staring out at the sea, enveloped in the fog and grey clouds that surrounded me, I was still in a state of shock from yesterday's revelation and the subsequent turn of events. I felt just as deflated as when I initially learned of it all those years ago. And here was my son, stripping away the lie that had been covered up out of shame and a sense of propriety. It had never occurred to me that Tommy knew. Never. And I felt so sad for him for having lost his father so many years before his actual death. All these years, him living with that knowledge, living with a lie, just like I. Now, I could only hope I had managed to persuade him to find forgiveness and that Jack would save Tommy and me from a possibly tragic future.

After breakfast yesterday, I sent Jimmy, Mary and Amy out to play so that Jack and I could sit Tommy down to have that conversation about the draft. The night before, on the news, there was a report of a battle involving about 100 Australians against some 1500 or 2000 Viet Cong in which the Australians astoundingly won. They beat them down and drove them back out of the village they were fighting in. Tommy, seeing the report, was enthusiastic, cheering for the allies and saying they were heroes, saying he couldn't wait to get over there and join the fight. He didn't seem to share my sentiments that this was not a just war, nor a war that could be won any time soon.

We tried to explain to him the horrors of jungle warfare with all its new weaponry and the untold numbers of men being maimed and killed or were now missing. I told him my fear that if he went over there, he wouldn't come back, that he would be killed. I also pointed out to him the discrepancies between what the government said and what the news media uncovered, that we were being lied to. I told him there were ways he could get out of going, that he could get a deferment and I started to tell him about what Sam had told me. In the middle of it, he jumped up and said, "Mom, I don't want to get out of going. I want to go fight for my country."

"Ok," I said, trying to remain unemotional about the whole thing. "Then join the Coast Guard. I am sure you could get in, with your love for the water and if there were any issue, I'm sure your uncle's service or even Jack's connections could help you get in. You would have a much better chance of survival in the Guard, than in the Army."

"No, Mom, I'm not taking the cowards way out. When I graduate, I'm going to enlist. I want to go fight for my country and I don't care if I have to die, at least I'll die a hero." He said this with such pride and conviction.

Not knowing what else to say, I continued to press the Coast Guard on him, telling him the advantages of that service and how he could make a career out of it and see the world.

"Mom, you are not listening. I am going to enlist in the Army and that's that. I'll be 18 and you can't stop me." He was angry now, and defiant, a behavior I had never seen in him.

"Tommy, in all your 17 years, you have never once argued with me or disregarded my wishes, so I am ordering you to join the Coast Guard." I was getting frantic, my heart was pounding and my voice was elevated when I said, "You will not disobey me."

He yelled right back at me, "I don't care what you say. You can't order me to do anything. This is my duty and for the honor of this family, I am going to enlist. I'm not a goddamned coward like my father, and I'll prove it."

I was stunned. In as calm a voice I could muster, I said, "Tommy, your father wasn't a coward. He lost his finger in a logging accident and they wouldn't take him."

He looked at me and laughed. "Cut the crap, Mom. You and I both know that's not true. That he chopped off his finger on purpose so he wouldn't have to go off to war."

I was shocked. How could he have known that? I was wracking my brain to think of some explanation for what he just said. "How do you know that?" I asked in disbelief.

"I was there that night. That night you heard it too. I got up to go to the bathroom and I was in the hallway. I heard that friend of his say it and Dad acknowledged it. I saw you slump down on the floor and cry. I was crying too but was too damned ashamed to even let you know I knew. I went back to my bed and cried my heart out. My father was a goddamned coward. But I am not my father. I swore right then and there I was going to be a soldier, whether there was a war or not, to make up for what he did. I have lived the last seven years with that festering inside me. And now, I am ready, willing and able to go to war, and by God, I am going to do that. And I'll be the best damned soldier there is or die trying."

I was mortified to think my little boy had heard that horrible truth. He was only ten. And he had lived with that lie all these years, never letting on that he knew. Sobbing, I managed to say, "Why didn't you tell me? I could have helped you to understand it, to not feel responsible for his sin."

"I saw how you picked yourself up and went on. I knew you were crying inside, but put up with him for us, for the sake of family. I decided to do the same thing. I put up with him, but I never forgot what he did."

I was at a loss for words and could barely look at Jack, feeling so much shame, but when I did look at him he had a loving look of consolation on his face. My expression must have said help because he jumped in with a new idea. "Tommy, if you're hellbent on going over there, and you don't want to go in the Guard, then at least choose a path that will increase your chances of survival. Go as a pilot. You can join the Navy or the Army or the Air Force, whichever you choose, they all have an air wing."

Tommy looked at him and didn't lash out and reject the idea. "I don't know the first thing about flying a plane. They won't take me in as a pilot."

"You've got eight months before you have to register and in that time, I can teach you to fly. I'm a certified instructor and I have a plane. And in the next eight months, I can teach you the fundamentals and get you almost 100 hours of flying time, if you're willing to do the work. With that knowledge and experience they would put you directly into flight school. They need pilots and how many guys that enlist do you think have flying experience?"

Tommy was thinking; I could imagine the wheels turning inside his head. At last, he said, "I never thought about being a pilot. If you think I can learn it, then, yeah, okay, being a pilot would be really cool."

"I know you can learn it. You're a smart kid. It's like learning how to drive a car, only you have to learn how the aircraft works, mechanically. Plus, there are a lot more gauges on the dashboard," he laughed as he said that last part. "So, do we have a deal?" Jack asked as he stuck out his hand.

"You bet," Tommy said and reached to shake his hand. Jack threw an arm around Tommy's shoulder and gave him a hug. Tears were streaming down my face in relief, though I still feared for his safety. Jack reached out his other arm and drew me to them and I hugged them both, so happy that my boy would be in far less danger and happy that Jack and Tommy had shared such a moment.

Tommy broke free, looked at Jack and said, "Thank you. Thank you for being more of a father to me than. . ." he stopped before saying what I knew he meant. He turned to look at me and said, "Mom, I'm sorry for the mean things I said, and for not telling you. I should have. Then you wouldn't have had to bear it alone."

"I could bear anything for your sake. I just wish you would have let me take away some of your pain. . .I can't even imagine how devastated you must have been. He was just my husband, but he was your father, your blood. But know this, Tommy, he didn't do it to hurt you, or me. And he regretted it for the rest of his life, that's why he drank. He couldn't live with what he'd done. So, feel sorry for him. He was scared. Men were dying all over the world and he'd just seen men torpedoed on a ship, blown up, drowned, badly burned. He was a young man, not much older than you and he had no father to guide him. And remember this, it took some amount of courage to stick his finger under that chain. So, forgive him. I have, many years ago."

Tommy threw his arms around me and hugged me tight and said, "I'll try." He whispered in my ear, "I love you, Mom," released me and started toward the door.

Jack called after him, "I might be gone when you get back, but I'll be here next weekend with books and charts and we can get started."

"Great. I'll be ready." After a few moments, he added, "Thanks, Dad," and left the house.

Port Orford 1967

As he promised, Jack showed up the next weekend with books and charts and they started their sessions. They'd spend hours learning the lessons, reviewing diagrams, with Jack quizzing Tommy on what he'd learned. At the end of every session, Jack would give Tommy homework to do during the week, to be followed by a test the following Saturday. Jimmy became interested too, telling Jack he wanted to learn as well. Thereafter, he would study the lessons with Tommy and quiz him to help him learn. Eventually, they went flying, with Tommy observing at first, but then actually doing, learning how to use his feet and then his hands, learning how to read the instruments. Jack said he was a natural, that he was picking it up easily.

Halloween came and went, then Thanksgiving, then Christmas and, before we knew it, we were celebrating Tommy's birthday. He was officially 18. Jack had been here almost every weekend, but the few times he missed, he would call Tommy and give him a new assignment and a quick quiz on the phone. I had never seen my son so committed to anything in school. He was hitting the books in earnest, both for Jack and his teachers, his report cards were much improved. And then he graduated, along with eleven of his classmates, which was around the average for this small town.

By this time, he was practically soloing in the plane. He had flown by himself with Jack by his side, correcting and suggesting better ways to handle things. He had done the takeoff and most recently brought the plane in for a landing, albeit a bit bumpy, but he had done it. Jack had given him sample exams which he passed with ease, and he had gotten in over 90 hours of flight time. He could become a certified private pilot right now if he wanted to, but of course, the military wanted him first. He had told Jack he wanted to join the Navy, which made Jack proud as can be, to think Tommy wanted to follow in his footsteps. He asked Jack to go with him to the recruiting office, not me, just Jack. I wasn't hurt or put out in any way, just happy that Tommy and Jack had developed such a close relationship, happy for both of them. Tommy had grown up so much in the time he spent with Jack and, miraculously, Jack hadn't had one nightmare since he started teaching Tommy to fly. I wasn't sure if it was due to Sam and his friends or whether it was the focus he had in teaching. Maybe Tommy reminded Jack of his former self, when he was young and ready to conquer the enemy all by himself. In either case, their relationship had been cathartic for both of them and to see them heading off to the recruiting office tugged at my heart. Jack was in his uniform, taking his son to a rite of passage. Tommy was about to cross the threshold of manhood and I couldn't have been prouder. Not surprisingly, he was accepted immediately with orders to be ready to report in two weeks; he would be notified where.

I heard the clinking of a knife on a glass, and was brought back to the room. Jack had brought the whole family out to dinner to celebrate Tommy's leaving the next day for Whidbey Island Naval Station in Washington. Jack was making a toast. "Let's raise our glasses to Tommy, who worked harder than anyone I've ever seen and is about to begin his life as a proud and brave Navy pilot. *'Non Sibi Sed Patriae'* or, in other words, *'Not for Self, but Country.'* To Tommy." We all raised our glasses to him and drank, though I could barely see him with the tears that were welling in my eyes.

"Well, how does it feel? Are you nervous?" I managed to ask my son.

"Yeah, I guess I am. Well, not really nervous. Anxious, I guess is a better word. New place, new people, strange bed. You know, stuff like that. I guess I won't be sleeping in any more, huh?"

Jack laughed and said, "That's for sure. I hope you like getting up at 5:30."

"You'll get used to that," I said, "but in many ways, it will still be like living home. Someone will cook for you and wash your clothes. It won't be all bad."

Jimmy chimed in, "Yeah, and you'll be sharing a room and a bathroom with forty or fifty other guys, not just me. And there's bound to be at least one snorer," he said jokingly. Despite his razzing, I knew Jimmy was going to really miss him. They'd shared the same room for seventeen years.

They were tossing barbs back and forth, even Mary joined in. I looked over at Amy, sitting next to Tommy, who was very quiet. She looked very sad, almost like she was going to cry, "Amy, don't be sad," I said, "Tommy is about to embark on one of the greatest accomplishments of his life."

"I know. But I'm going to miss him," she said, barely holding back the tears. I wanted to grab her up in my arms and hold her, but Tommy, beat me to it. He gave her a hug and said, "I'm counting on you to write to me every week and tell me what these two knuckleheads are up to. Will you do that?"

"Of course. I didn't know you could have mail there. Mom, do you know his address?" she asked me.

"No, but Tommy will let us know as soon as he gets there," I assured her.

"Yes, I will," Tommy told her. "I'll write you a letter and tell you where to send your letters. But only if you promise you're not going to be sad. This is something I really want to do and I want you to be happy for me, okay, Squirt?"

She promised and the dinner progressed with lots of joking and kidding, and Jimmy badgering Jack to know when his flying lessons would start. I was savoring every moment knowing full well that it would be a very long time before we were all together again. Until finally Jack said, "I think it's time we went home and went to bed. We have an early start in the morning."

At home, in bed, I snuggled into Jack's arms and said, "I think tomorrow will be the hardest day of my life. That little boy saved me from a life without love. Early on, I realized that my husband was emotionally deficient, that I would never have a loving, deeply satisfying marriage. But Tommy gave me all the love I needed and wanted. He nurtured me, just as I did him. He would cuddle with me and laugh and just give me so much pleasure. He's done that his whole life, no matter what, he has always been there for me, with the right words or the right actions. And now I have to say goodbye to him as he heads off into the world without me to watch over him," I said tearily.

"Don't worry, he's going to be just fine. He really has good instincts and I've seen him tap into it. Many times, I put him in precarious situations and he always found the right way out," Jack assured me. "Besides, you have me to cuddle with, and nurture and give you pleasure."

I snickered at his subtlety and found myself drawn into the warmth and sensuousness of his kiss.

We'd settled into a routine without Tommy in the house. His absence was definitely felt but we heard from him quite often. Many letters were flying back and forth between here and Whidbey Island. He'd been there almost six months and with each letter he sounded more confident, more mature. He'd made some friends at the school and he was learning lots. He said flying an F-4 fighter jet was a lot different than flying Jack's Cessna, but that the principles were the same and he was getting the hang of it. Carrier training—learning to take off and land on an aircraft carrier—was still to come, but he would be graduating to that soon.

Meanwhile, Jimmy was eating it up. Between Tommy's letters, the nightly news, and his own flight instruction with Jack, he was very "gung ho," to use one of his favorite words. He was far more gregarious than Tommy and bragged about his new-found skill. I loved my second son dearly, but wouldn't tolerate his glorification of being a fighter pilot. Yes, it was a necessity and becoming a fighter pilot was something to be very proud of. But, war was awful and very dangerous and I spent a lot of time and energy pointing that out to him. Whatever horrific images of the war I could find, I made sure he saw them, like an issue of *LIFE* magazine that covered the "blunt reality of war," in graphic photos. He soon changed his attitude. He cried in my arms when he saw the mothers and their dead babies, the large number of innocent civilians being killed and maimed and dead soldiers, young men just like him. The full brutality and devastation of war finally sunk in, along with the responsibility he would be assuming in an effort to end the war as quickly as possible. That was the only way I could help him make sense of it, to tell him that if he had to go, if he had to be part of it, he could make a difference as a pilot, to help wipe out the enemy and end the war, saving lives, both civilian and military. His thinking changed, almost overnight. He wasn't a kid anymore, though he was only seventeen.

In September, we heard reports of two local boys being killed, both Marines, one from Gold Beach and the other from Bandon. They'd been ambushed and pinned down for days in something called Operation Swift. It went on for eleven days, with 127 killed and twice as many wounded—it wasn't swift enough for those young boys. Losing two men from so close by, brought the reality of war right into our home. My heart broke for those mothers. I identified with them having been forced to give up their sons, just as I would very soon. Amy and I went to a memorial service for the young man from Bandon and marched in the protest led by his family, carrying placards demanding "Peace Now" and "Bring our Boys Home." It was peaceful and somber, and in the grand scheme of things, quite small and insignificant, not like the rallies in big cities. But for once, I felt like I had a voice, that even though we wouldn't make the news, our message would at least be heard by local people and others passing through. Amy and I had our own little grassroots movement going, writing letters to newspaper editors, posting signs in local businesses, trying to incite others to take up the cause and protest to our senators and representatives, even the President, with letters or marches. I prayed every day for peace, that it would happen before my boys ever set foot in Vietnam.

Then once again, war hit home. A young man from our own town was killed in what was called the "Tet Offensive." We watched the news coverage in disbelief. Our government and military commanders had been telling us "we are winning over there," "we are on the offensive," "we are making steady progress." They talked about "kill ratios" and "body counts" and how the Communists were unable to mount a major offensive. But here we were, seeing how untrue that was. The Communists had mounted a massive attack. With an estimated 80,000 troops, they had attacked more than a hundred towns and cities within a matter of days. They executed thousands of civilians and thousands of our young men were lost, including this boy from Port Orford, whose family I knew well. But even more horrifying to me, were the reports of downed aircraft. I had deluded myself into thinking my boys would be immune from death by being in a plane, but realized now how wrong I had been. They were less likely to be killed up in the air, but they were not immune.

Throughout America, the tide changed after this battle. People felt they had been lied to, betrayed. All across the country, people were marching. There was a public outcry to end the war, not just from civilians, but celebrities and Congressmen, who were being badgered by their constituents.

Tommy didn't have much more training to go, before the year was up, he would be deployed. I prayed harder and wrote more letters—that was all that was in my power to do.

*

Our country was in shambles, with dissention everywhere. There were more race riots, anti-war protests, even a hippie movement that was against anything the establishment offered. And while none of it actually happened in Port Orford, the tension was in the air. I heard it every day at CJ's, people talking about the news, what they'd seen, what they'd read, what they'd heard. Bad news kept pouring out of Vietnam and then the unthinkable happened. Two of our great leaders who held the promise of unifying this country were assassinated, struck down by hatred and fear. Martin Luther King Jr., a minister and champion of black people everywhere, who preached civil disobedience through non-violence and did more to advance the rights of blacks, was shot down in April. Then, only two months later, Bobby Kennedy, who was running for president on an anti-war platform, who vowed to right the perilous path our country and its leadership were on, was taken from us by a Palestinian, who feared Kennedy's pro-Israel stance. Hatred and fear were running rampant in this country, along with mistrust, especially of our government. Like me, people felt powerless and skeptical of anything coming out of Washington. There were rumors of an atrocity in Vietnam, of our own soldiers killing civilians, unofficially, of course. So much of what we saw on the TV news and read in the newspapers had an "otherworldly" quality to it. Living here in such a small white town, so isolated on the farthest fringe of the United States, it was hard to identify with so much of it.

Tommy's letters continued to remain upbeat. He was excited about all he was learning, though I doubted he would tell me if he was discouraged or afraid in any way. In a matter of days, he would be going through his final trials and, if he passed, and he was sure he would, he would be given his flight wings and be ready to join the ranks and be deployed. Jack promised to fly us up there for the ceremony once we knew when it was. I was both anxious and frightened at the idea, because I didn't want Tommy to go over there for one thing, and I'd never been up in a plane before. But driving there and back would take days and be exhausting, so Jack suggested that we fly and did his best to assure me it was safe.

*

I remember waking up in a hospital room, with an IV in my arm. I felt a lot of weight on top of me. Lots of blankets, I could hardly move my legs. I was cold. I was alone. I tried to remember how I got here, but felt like I was in the midst of a heavy fog. I looked for the button to call the nurse and pressed it. Jack. Where was Jack? He was beside me in the. . .the plane. We had been in his plane, and then it all started to come back to me.

The day started out early. We had gotten up, showered and dressed, then had a quick breakfast with the girls. Mary and Amy were sorry they couldn't come with us, but understood the space constraints. I gave them instructions about food and staying close to home, locking up for the night, all the stuff mothers worry about, but also knowing my kids were responsible and that they were old enough to take care of themselves. I kissed them goodbye, promising to call as soon as we landed and we left in Jack's car for the drive to the airport.

His plane sat ready for us, having been refueled and moved for takeoff. Jack helped me up and in and belted me down. He got in and handed me a list to read to him, item by item, as he did all the pre-flight checks. He handed me a headset to put on and tested that we could hear each other. He was speaking to someone to get permission for takeoff and once granted, we started to move. I remember feeling anxious, wondering how I was going to feel, once up in the air, but stayed calm and open to the experience. After all, Tommy, Jimmy and Jack all loved to fly. When we moved down to the end of the runway, Jack stopped, flipped a few switches and knobs, and I felt the engines getting louder and louder and then giving me a nod and a smile, and one last squeeze of my hand, we started moving, faster and faster and faster still. I felt myself being pushed back against my seat, then the plane wobbled a little and I realized we had left the ground and were climbing. We were going higher, though my stomach was still on the ground. I looked out my window and we were over the ocean, making a turn to the north and going higher and higher. I heard in my ears, "We're going to take an ocean route, I think it will be prettier. Then when we get to the Olympic Peninsula, we can fly east to Whidbey. It will be about 4 hours of flight time. Okay?" I nodded to him and smiled.

Eventually, we stopped climbing and the plane leveled out. I felt a thud and looked at Jack.

"I just stowed the wheels. Nothing to worry about. You alright?" he asked.

"Fine," I said, no doubt, unconvincingly. "It's pretty amazing being up here. The view is spectacular." And it was. The skies were clear and very blue with lots of sunshine. I felt the wind now and then, causing the plane to wobble, but it was mostly smooth, though the sound was deafening. I fully understood why we were wearing headsets, though I had never thought about that before.

We weren't too far from shore and the view was amazing. I was seeing places I had never seen before: thousands of acres of trees, rugged cliffs plunging down into the ocean, miles and miles of sandy beaches and sea stacks of all sizes dotting the coastline. The Oregon coast was geologically captivating. Looking down into the ocean I saw whales and, on the rocks, cadres of seals and sea lions. Eventually, I got used to the sound and that quivering in my body from the vibration of the engine.

After an hour or so, I fully relaxed and was truly enjoying being up in the air, feeling light and free, untethered from the earth. I was pointing out a lighthouse to Jack when the plane shuddered and felt different. I looked at Jack and he was looking at his dials. He flicked one of them and said, "We have a problem. We're losing oil pressure."

"Can you fix it?" I asked, trying to keep the panic from my voice.

"Not up here. We're going to have to land," he said and reached for his map. He was studying it when I sensed we were slowing and dropping lower in the sky. "Damn," he said as he tossed the map into the back. "We're too far from any airport. We won't make it. I'm going to have to set it down in the water. Here, put this on." He handed me some kind of a flotation device. He was cool as a cucumber but he must have seen the look of panic on my face. "Don't worry, I can put it down gently and I'll get us as close to shore as possible." He was calm, amazingly calm, as he turned the plane toward land. I put on the vest while he radioed a mayday. He was trying to reach air traffic control. They heard him. He gave them coordinates as we continued to drop lower in the sky. I noticed the water getting closer as did the shore, but we were still at least a mile out. I prayed the engine would keep running till we got close enough. And then it stopped. The noise stopped. The vibration stopped. We were coasting.

Jack took off his headset and reached to remove mine. "Look, when we hit the water, you're going to feel it, but as long as you're strapped in, you should be fine." He grabbed my hand. "Don't worry, they're coming for us. We won't be in the water long." He went back to flying the plane, using the wing flaps to slow us down and keeping the nose pulled up. He was totally focused and his brow was furrowed. I could only imagine what was going through his mind, as I fearfully remembered my kids and worked to quash the thought that I would never see them again. The seconds seemed like hours as we continued to drop lower, but the shore was coming closer. I prayed he could keep the plane out of the water long enough for us to get really close to shore. I felt like we were in slow motion and it was quiet except for the sound of us slicing through the air and then I felt a bump. "Hold on." Jack yelled as he tried to land the plane softly. He kept the plane level as we continued to plow forward through the water, until we stopped. There was silence. Both of us sitting there, waiting for something to happen. Nothing did, we were just bobbing there for what seemed like minutes, but was really only seconds. Then we heard water rushing in. My feet were wet. "I want you to take off your shoes. When you open the door, get out on the wing and pull the tabs on the vest. Stay there holding on as long as you can. I'll come around and get you," Jack ordered as he pulled on his vest. "We're going to be fine, I promise. I won't let anything happen to us," he said as we stared into each other's eyes. The water was getting higher inside the plane. "Now go."

I pulled on the door handle and pushed it out with my shoulder and water, ice-cold water, flooded in. I pulled myself out onto the wing which was already under water. I tried to do what Jack told me. Stay put. Hold on. My feet were numb and the chill was running up my legs like an electric current. Soon the water was over my knees, the plane was going down. "Let go and come into the water to me," Jack said. He was behind me. The water was so cold. I didn't want to get in, but I knew in a matter of seconds, the plane would be far below the water anyway. I let go and dropped in. I felt Jack grab me and pulled me into him. I was shivering and trying to hold on. "Kick your feet. Try to kick your feet," he said as his teeth chattered. I tried, but I couldn't seem to move. I felt him tugging on me. And then I felt nothing, as if I had slipped below the water and floated there. I saw Jack. And Tommy, Jimmy, Mary and Amy. And then black.

There was a doctor standing over me, taking my pulse. "Open," he said as he slipped a thermometer in my mouth. "Welcome back, Jennifer. I'm Doctor Carver," he said as he looked at a device in his hands. It beeped and he removed the thermometer. "You're doing just fine. Your temperature is almost back to normal."

"Where's Jack?" I asked. "Is he alright?"

"Yes, Jack is doing fine. He's in a room down the hall, and has just come back to consciousness. As soon as his temperature stabilizes, we'll let you two have a visit."

"What day and time is it?" I had the presence of mind to ask.

"It's Saturday evening. Just about 7."

I realized we were so long overdue, and remembered my promise to call home. "My kids. I have to call my kids," I shrieked as I tried to get up.

He pushed me back down and said calmly, "I'll have a nurse come in and help you with that. I want you to stay underneath those covers a while longer. And I'll be back in an hour. If you need anything else, just ask the nurse."

He left and in a few minutes a nurse walked in to the side of the bed, where there was a phone. She asked me for the phone number and made the call, holding the receiver by my ear. I quickly asked her where I was. Amy answered the phone frantically. "It's Mom, Amy. I just wanted to tell you we are fine." She was crying and hysterically asking me why I didn't call sooner. I explained to her in a few words what had happened and apologized for not calling sooner, for scaring her and her sister and brothers. She told me Tommy had called hours ago to say we hadn't shown up. They were all worried. "I'm sorry I didn't call sooner, but I just woke up here and you were my first thought." I asked her to get in touch with Tommy and Jimmy and for them all to sit tight. I would call again when I knew more. I asked the nurse to give Amy the phone number to reach me. I told her I loved her, loved them all and said goodbye.

The nurse asked if I wanted anything, and I said, "Yes, my Jack."

*

The doctor had been in to tell me my temperature was almost normal and at my request removed some of the blankets—I was hot. I was feeling a bit more like myself but I hurt all over. The Doctor told me it was a reaction to the accident and gave me something to ease the aching. I asked again about Jack and he told me he was doing fine and I would see him soon. Soon. That's a relative term. Soon could be minutes, hours, or days. I could see street lights on outside, and knew that it was nighttime. I was still trying to remember how we had gotten here to the hospital. My memory ended shortly after getting in the cold water. I remembered Jack telling me to kick, but that was all. Then I woke up here a few hours ago. Just then my door opened and in came Jack, in a wheelchair with blankets wrapped around him. I was never so happy to see anyone, and tears filled my eyes. He was pale, but smiling at me with his blue eyes and colorless lips as he rolled closer to my bed. I wanted to jump into his arms but when I tried to get up, I found it so hard to move.

"Stay there, Jenny," he said as he took my hand in his. He was beaming at me and I could see his eyes were watery too.

"We make quite the couple," I said with a chuckle.

"Yes, we do," he said and turned serious. "I am so sorry, Jenny. I hope you can forgive me."

"There's nothing to forgive. You didn't intentionally make the engine quit. And I know you saved me in the water or I wouldn't be here. I must have blacked out because I don't remember, and yet I am here, alive and well. For the most part," I said jokingly. "Please don't blame yourself."

"I've been flying planes for over 20 years and other than being shot down, I've never had to ditch a plane. Even when there was engine trouble, I've always been able to land the thing and walk away. I don't understand what could have happened. I had the plane serviced before I left LA." He paused and I could see his mind spinning and he looked confused and worried, and cold.

"Stop punishing yourself. Please. We're both okay, that is all that matters," I touched his cheek and smiled at him. I wanted to get his mind off the crash and said, "I called home. The girls know we are okay and I asked them to get in touch with the boys. They were worried sick. They just want to know when we're coming home."

He perked up at the mention of the kids and home. "I've made arrangements for a car, when we get released, which hopefully will be in the morning. We could get to Whidbey Island by Monday, if you want to see Tommy before he leaves."

"Oh, can we?" I was elated at the prospect of seeing my son. I didn't care about the crash, or almost drowning or hypothermia, only that I missed seeing my son. Jack seemed happy at seeing me happy, but I noticed he was shivering. I moved over in the bed and said, "Why don't you climb in here with me and let me make you warm." He smiled and did just that. I spooned his back to my front and wrapped my arm around him. He felt cold, but I knew that my body heat would warm him quickly, just as it had with Tommy all those years ago.

194

After a few minutes, he stopped shivering and we lay there, happy to be alive and together, and soon I felt his breathing slow. He was asleep. I thought about seeing my son and how happy I was to be here in this bed with this man and next thing I knew it was morning.

*

The doctor released us in the morning, each wearing a set of hospital scrubs and slippers, with instructions to not do anything too strenuous as our bodies needed rest to fully recover. A taxicab took us to a car rental place where Jack's office had arranged for us to pick up a car. From there, we drove to a bank, where money had been wired to Jack by his company. With both a car and cash, our next stop was a department store, where we each bought street clothes and shoes. Already exhausted, we headed to the Interstate for the long drive north to Seattle, where we would get the ferry over to the island. We had talked to the girls and Tommy earlier this morning to tell them our plans and Tommy knew we would be on base tomorrow morning. He would try to get his brother cut loose from his training and bring him along.

It was a long drive and there was lots of time for Jack to tell me the harrowing story of our rescue from the cold waters of the Pacific Ocean. He swam with one arm, dragging me closer and closer to shore. He feared I would die in those waters and said that was what drove him to keep going. He'd gotten us to about a half mile from shore when a Coast Guard chopper approached and a diver dropped into the ocean not far from us. He swam to us and when a rescue stretcher was lowered, he managed to get both of us into it. Once inside the helicopter, they wrapped us in blankets, recovered the diver and flew us to the Coast Guard Station where an ambulance waited to take us to the hospital. Jack said he was barely conscious, shivering violently and once he knew I was alive, he blacked out, until he woke in the hospital, hours later. He told me we'd been in the water over an hour and was very thankful the Coast Guard showed up when they did. He also told me his office was making arrangements to try to salvage the plane; he wanted to know what had gone wrong with the engine.

About half way to Seattle, Jack pulled off the highway in search of food. We found a diner, not too far off the road, and the parking lot was pretty full, always a good sign. We were seated in a booth and ordered hot tea, both of us needing the caffeine to try to stay awake. Though we were both feeling tired, we had quite a long way to go. The waitress brought our tea and we ordered our combined lunch and dinner.

Jack reached across the table and took both my hands in his. "Jenny, this ordeal has made me realize something. I am mortal. That at any moment, on any trip, whether in my plane or in my car, I could be killed, and you would be left alone, to struggle through life, working hard to provide for yourself and the kids, our kids, and I don't want that. I want to take care of you, our family, always. And so, when I get back to LA, I'm going to see my lawyer and make you the beneficiary of my estate. My business, my house, my wealth, whatever I have will be yours, if anything should happen to me."

"Jack, stop. I don't want to think about anything happening to you."

"I know and I don't want you to think about it. I'm just telling you what I plan to do. And so there is never any question about your legal right to my estate, I want us to get married. And soon."

He stopped and I just stared at him as he continued, "I want you to be my wife and I want your kids to be my kids, legally. I want us to be a family in the eyes of the state. Say you'll marry me."

"Of course, I'll marry you," I said as I squeezed his hands. "Even though I feel like you are my husband and the father to my children already. But I, too, was thinking last night that if anything were to happen to me, my kids would be left to fend for themselves. My brother is my only relative and he hasn't been part of our life for so many years, and with his drinking, I don't know if I could count on him to take care of them. I would be thrilled to have you as the legal guardian of my kids because I know you would raise them as I would." I laughed and said, "Though, far more affluently."

We reached our bodies across the table and kissed, then settled down to eat our food, chatting throughout about when and where we might have the ceremony. Like two love-struck teenagers, we were making plans for our wedding, which we agreed would be simple, at the house, with our girls as attendants. We were both sad that Tommy and Jimmy would not be there. We would see Tommy tomorrow and then he was shipping out to somewhere in Southeast Asia. He didn't know where, but no doubt, he would be on one of the carriers for which he'd been training for months and was now certified for duty. My son, a Navy pilot. It was amazing to me, more than I ever dreamed for him. I kept thinking of the baby in my arms and all he had meant to me. The little boy whose nose I blew and nicked knees I'd bandaged, who'd almost died at sea, now all grown up, no longer a boy, a young man, who had learned to fly a million-dollar fighting machine and was about to go off to war. I felt proud as can be, but was also scared. I knew there were no guarantees that he would be safe. He could still be shot down and killed or taken prisoner. I prayed that his wits and instincts would keep him alive and that he would always be in the right place at the right time. Jimmy, too. Maybe this horrible war would come to an end before he ever had to leave.

For the first time, I knew what it must have been like for my father, watching his son go off to war, not knowing if he would come back whole or if he would ever see him again, which made me think of my brother. How I wished he was coming with us to see Tommy off, but we barely had any relationship at all. I hadn't seen him in many years, hardly ever talked to him, despite my efforts to keep him in my life. I sent cards, letters, pictures of the kids, but would never get anything back. Once in a while he would call to thank me, but the conversation was always short. I'd invited him to come visit numerous times, but he always declined. Too busy, couldn't get away. Always the excuse.

"Should we get back on the road?" Jack was asking me.

I snapped out of my thoughts and said, "Sure, I think I can handle a few more hours in the car. But I'll be glad to curl up in bed tonight. It's been a long day."

"It's not too much farther," he said as he wrapped his arm around me and led me to the car.

*

On our way back home, I'd asked Jack to stop in Portland, so I could see my brother. Ever since that tearful goodbye with Tommy and Jimmy, I felt this great need to see Frank. I wanted him back in my life, to be my friend, as he had been when we were kids. I had such fond memories of our childhood spent together: swimming in the lake, building forts on the beach with the driftwood that floated ashore, going to the movies on Saturday afternoon, listening to the radio at night, *Fibber McGee and Molly* was our favorite. He always watched over me, made sure nothing bad ever happened to me. Once so close, and now, we were estranged. He didn't seem to want to see me, but I wanted to make sure he was alright, that nothing bad was happening to him.

We got to his apartment where he'd been living since his divorce, but when I knocked and the door opened, there was a young woman holding a child. She said she'd been living there for four months and didn't know my brother. Disappointed, we found a phone booth and I looked in the directory for his business address, then found it on the city map. We drove there, but there was a sign in the door that read "Closed." I went to the door and looked inside. It was dark inside except for a light in the back and there was someone moving around back there. I tried the door; it was locked, so I started banging on the door and calling Frank's name. The person turned to look at me and it was Frank. He stared at me for a few seconds and then started toward me. It was dim inside but I could see

200

he was unkempt. He unlocked the door, opened it and said with a smile, "Jenny. Hi. What are you doing here?"

I tried not to show the concern and worry on my face. This was not the brother I remembered, who came home from the war so young and healthy, vibrant and ready to take on the world. Now, he was skinny but bloated, wearing dirty clothes, messy hair, needing a shave, and smelly, both from body odor and alcohol. He was drunk and looking at me with blood-shot eyes.

"We've come to see you," I managed to say in as friendly a tone as possible. "We were passing through and I wanted you to meet my friend. Can we come in?"

"Well sure, come on in," he said carrying a coffee mug and leading us into an office where there was a small sofa and two chairs besides the desk. "Have a seat."

Jack and I sat on the sofa while he sat in one of the chairs facing us, sipping from his mug, which I could smell did not contain coffee. I introduced Jack, who reached over to shake my brother's hand. I had dozens of questions and didn't know where to start, so said, "We stopped at your apartment before coming here."

"Yeah, I don't live there anymore," he said, stating the obvious.

I sat there trying to remain calm. I could not believe this was my brother. He was a down-and-out drunk, with a distended belly; he probably had already poisoned his liver. How had this happened to him and why did I not know? I was angry at his wife for not letting me know. I was angry at myself for not pursuing him when he continually declined my invitations.

"Seemed silly to be paying rent there, when I had this room set up here. I used to stay here when I was working on a big project," he said as his voice trailed off like he was remembering. "I'll be ready for the next big project when it comes."

I knew there would be no "next big project." It was Tuesday morning. The office should have been open; he should be groomed and dressed nicely. . .and sober.

"You said you were passing through, where to?" He was trying desperately to appear normal and cohesive, when he was anything but.

"We're heading back home. We were up in Washington, on Whidbey Island. We went to see Tommy off. You remember, my oldest son. He's in the Navy and just finished his flight training. He left today for Vietnam." I said as cheerily as I could, looking for signs of recognition and understanding but there were none.

"That's nice," was all he could say. He was staring at my face, then lifted his cup to his lips and drained it.

I looked at Jack and whispered for him to leave us. He rose and told Frank he had to get something from his car and walked out. I was on the verge of tears and wracking my brain for what to say and do for my brother. Maybe I could get him to come with us. Maybe get him into rehab, get him sober, make him healthy again; he could live with us and I could take care of him.

In as calm and upbeat a voice I could muster, I said, "Frank, it doesn't look like there's too much going on here, why don't you come back with us. The girls would love to see you and you'd enjoy being back in Port Orford. It hasn't changed very much, still slow, there's no stress, and the air is clean there, you could enjoy the outdoors: hiking, beachcombing, fishing. And I could cook for you, like I used to when it was just you, me and Pa. It looks like you could stand some good cooking."

"No. Thanks, Jenny. But I can't leave here. I'm too busy," he said and I wondered if he actually believed that.

And then, I lost my cool. "Frank, if you were busy, this office would be open, not with dust all over every surface." I was yelling, with tears rolling down my cheeks. "You'd be washed and dressed and shaved and you wouldn't be drinking booze at 11 o'clock in the morning." I lowered my voice and went to kneel next to him. "Frank, let me help you, you need to stop this drinking and get healthy and get your life back together. Please. I can't bear to see you like this."

He was crying now, too. "Leave me be, Jenny. I don't want to get healthy, I don't want to live, I don't deserve to live, I just want to live inside this bottle until I die. Now just go on home and let me be."

"Why, Frank, why? You have so much to live for. You have two kids who need their father. You have a sister who needs her brother, and nieces and nephews who need their uncle. We all need you in our lives. Please let me take you to rehab."

"No. I don't want to live anymore." Between his crying and his drunkenness, I could barely understand what he was saying. "I can't live with my guilt anymore. I killed people, I killed an innocent man. I deserve to die. I deserve to die."

I didn't understand what he was talking about, so I asked, "What people? What are you talking about?"

"In the war. In Iceland. We were ordered there to roust the Nazis that had taken over a research installation. When we got close to the buildings, they came storming out, guns blazing. We were under attack, shooting anything that moved. I kept firing. Then there was movement on my right flank, so I fired. A man went down. And when it was over, they were all dead. I went over to the man. He was a civilian, a native. He was lying in a pool of blood. I had killed him. An innocent man. Every time I close my eyes, I see him. Dead. In the blood." He was sobbing and I held him, feeling so much sorrow for him. I wanted to take away his pain, but didn't really know the right words.

"Frank, listen. It was war. Your government sent you over there, they gave you the gun and taught you how to use it. They ordered you to that spot and told you to kill. You were following orders. For your country. The Nazis were taking away people's freedom. You were there to rescue it, preserve it. And this man you think is innocent was no doubt a collaborator, or why would he be there at all. If he were innocent, he would be cowering inside. He might have had a gun. He might have been there to kill you. You are not to blame for his death. You must believe that and stop punishing yourself. . .and everyone who loves you. Please, I am begging you, come to rehab with me. You need to stop destroying yourself and get well. Your kids need you. They need their father. You may have taken lives over there, under orders, but don't take more lives here. Yours. And your kids."

I stopped to wipe away his tears. I knew he was listening to me, so I went on. "The best way for you to overcome any sense of guilt that you may feel is to atone for it. You can't bring that man back to life, but you can make someone else's life better. You can give back. And you can start with your kids. They need a father. They need your love, your guidance, your presence."

"No. I tried. They don't want any part of me. They told me so," he said, so defeated.

"That's probably true. They don't want any part of a drunk. But if you get sober and get your life back on track, they will talk to you and they will listen. You'll have to tell them the truth and you'll have to ask for their forgiveness, but children need their father, whether he's perfect or not. Please, do this for them. Say you'll come with me."

He sat there holding on to me, just as I was holding onto him. And finally, so softly I could hardly hear him, he said, "Okay."

I hugged him harder and kissed his forehead, then remembered Jack. "You know, Frank, you are not the only one who has those memories and nightmares. Jack was a prisoner of war, held by the Japanese for over a year under barbarous conditions. He saw things, had things done to him and did things to others that he had trouble confronting. He turned to drink as well. But someone kicked him in the butt just like I'm doing with you. He quit drinking and got his life back on track. Now he has a successful business and a family who loves him. And he's been talking with other vets who are suffering, like he was. Like you are. I'm going to go get him and you can spend some time together while I go make some arrangements. Okay?"

"Okay, but sis, please can I have a drink? I'm shaking. Just a little one. Please."

"Of course," I said as I helped him up off the floor and into a chair. "I know you need it."

I went to get Jack and told him quickly what had transpired. I asked him to talk with him and to get him a shot. Then I got on the phone with the Veterans Association and begged for them to take him today. They were full they said; he could be admitted in two or three weeks. I tried to explain that that wouldn't work. That he might be dead in two weeks. Still, the woman on the other end of the phone said she was sorry, but they were full, he'd have to go on a waiting list.

"Listen. This man went to war when his country asked him. He volunteered to go. He willingly put his life in harm's way when his country needed him. He didn't ask them to wait. He went right away. He went into battle. He was shot at and almost killed. And he killed people, that haunt him to this day. For over 20 years, he's been suffering with the pain of having killed people. For his country. So, please, I am begging you, let his country help him now. He's finally agreed to go, to get help. If you don't take him today, he'll go right back into that bottle and he won't ever come out. Please," I managed to get out, through my sobbing.

I heard papers rustling and was so afraid she was going to say no or, worse yet, just hang up on me. I was trying to think of what else I could possibly say to convince her. I wanted her to feel sorry for me—maybe she had a brother she loved or lost, and could sympathize with me. At last, she came back on the line and said, "Alright. If you bring him today, we'll find a place for him. What is his name?"

I told her and thanked her profusely. She told me where to take him and we hung up. When I went back to Frank, he was showered and dressed and looked so much better. Jack was helping him with his shoes. "The VA has agreed to take you today and they are right here in Portland. So, when you are ready, we can go."

"I guess I'm as ready as I'm ever going to be," he said as he got up from the chair.

I smiled and gave him a hug and said, "Then, let's be on our way."

*

On that long car ride home, Jack got us talking about the wedding again, for which I was grateful. Having a wedding to think about over the next two weeks was far better than thinking about my brother and what he would endure over the coming month. He couldn't have visitors during that time, so all I would be able to do was call the facility to check on his status. Over the many miles, we made many decisions about our big day and before we knew it, were back in Port Orford.

We'd arrived home to the loving welcome of our girls who'd been alone for four days—except for a few check-ins by CJ—and had survived nicely. Cooking and cleaning up after themselves and staying safe, I was proud of them and, needless to say, they were thrilled when they heard our news about the wedding. We spent the next two weeks making dresses and arrangements for flowers and a minister, sending invitations to a few friends from town, getting blood tests and, lastly, drove to Gold Beach for a marriage license.

My first order of business, though, had been to get in touch with my sister-in-law and tell her about Frank. She was friendly and appreciative but said she was involved with another man—one who didn't drink. She said she would be happy to visit him when he was allowed visitors but couldn't be part of his life beyond that. And Frank had been right, his kids wanted nothing to do with him, at first. I talked to each of them a few times, getting to know them first to win their trust (I hadn't seen them since they were little girls.) Eventually, I convinced them that his alcoholism was a result of his war experience and that their support was vital to his recovery. One of his girls was in nursing school, so was more willing to accept that explanation. She persuaded her sister and they both agreed to see him, if I would go with them, which I promised to do once I got the go-ahead from the VA.

But today was my wedding day, and just as it had been twenty years ago, it was a beautiful sunny day with a gentle breeze. Amy and Mary were stunning in their pink dresses, wearing crowns of pink flowers with matching bouquets. We paired Mary as my maid of honor, with CJ who was Jack's best man. (Over the years, they had become good friends and CJ was thrilled to have been asked.) Amy was with Ned, the only other man in town who knew both of us. I truly wished my boys were here to share the day, but they belonged to the Navy at the present.

I think weddings make us feel a bit maudlin, make you think about all the people you wish could be there but weren't, like my Mom and Pa, and Frank. And Verna, who'd been such a good friend over the years; she had met a man last year who was crazy about her and her kids and now lived in Washington state. And then I remembered Jane, and how when we were teenagers we fantasized about our weddings, about what we would wear with one as bride and the other as maid of honor. Where once we'd been inseparable, I hadn't seen her now in over twenty years. We'd stayed in touch with letters, cards and an occasional phone call, but she had no reason to come back here, as her father had died years ago, and her mother now lived with her in Hawaii. I lamented the loss of that friendship and knew then she was just part of my past, like so many others. So today, my best friends were my girls and for that I was happy, not sad.

I was about to be formally married to a man I loved with all my heart, who made me feel more loved than I had ever felt in my entire life—our souls were entwined. I felt a connection to this man the first time I met him, all those years ago, though it was not something I could really explain. I thought then it was just a girlhood crush, just a feeling, a sense of familiarity, of belonging, that I could find no words to describe. Today, he and I were being publicly, legally bound in this ceremony, though in our hearts and minds, we'd been bound as husband and wife for many years.

I finished pinning a garland of baby pink roses through my hair to match the simple, palest pink sheath dress I wore. I was surprised that I was a little nervous, like a young bride. How silly I thought—I was a widow with grown children. Just then Mary walked in, with Amy beside her, and asked if I was ready. "I guess I am. Do I look alright?" I asked.

"Mom, you look beautiful," Mary said, with Amy in agreement. We had a three-way hug.

"Let's not keep them waiting then," I said and we left the house, out onto the walkway. Mary's boyfriend was in charge of the music and started the wedding march. I took a deep breath and we started to walk slowly toward the minister, on the bluff overlooking the ocean, where CJ and Ned stood, side by side, next to Jack, who was resplendent in a black suit, white shirt and dazzling pink striped tie. He was so handsome, I couldn't take my eyes from him. When we reached him, both girls gave me a kiss on the cheek. I handed my bouquet to Mary and took Jack's hands in mine. He gave them a little squeeze and I squeezed right back. The music faded away and the Minister began his speech about the sanctity of marriage. Half listening to him, I was so enthralled with Jack's eyes and his smile and elated to be standing before him, just looking at him, feeling his love. And then, he was speaking, repeating the words of the vow the Minister was saying, placing a simple gold ring he had chosen on my finger and promising to love, cherish and honor till death do us part. When Jack said "I do," I felt my heart burst with joy. Then it was my turn. I repeated the vow, placed a gold band on his finger and with all my heart said, "I do." Jack pulled me to him and gave me the sweetest kiss I had ever felt, one that made me tingle right down to my toes. I hadn't thought that I could love this man any more than I already did, but suddenly I felt my love grow inside, in a way I didn't think was possible.

We were now man and wife in the eyes of the world and the law. Our guests gathered around with hugs and kisses and offers of congratulations. Champagne and seltzer water were served, and CJ made a heartwarming toast to Jack and me. We posed for a wedding photo, then cut our cake and shared it all around. One by one, our guests came to wish us well and take their leave. It had been a beautiful day shared with people we cared about, but happy as I was, there was an underlying sadness that my boys and my brother weren't here to share it with us.

*

Within a few weeks, being told my brother could have a family visit, I made the arrangements with his daughters for the following weekend, as they were both in school. When I walked into his room and got my first glimpse of him, I felt my heart leap. He looked so much better than the day we brought him here—he actually looked healthy. I gave him a big hug and a kiss and told him how happy I was to see him and how proud I was of him. Jack shook his hand and greeted him with some words of encouragement as well. Frank then noticed his girls standing behind us by the door. I beckoned them to me and holding their hands, said to my brother, "I am sure you have some things to talk about with your girls, so Jack and I are going to leave you for a bit and go find some coffee." The girls looked a little leery, but I patted them each on the shoulder to reassure them and we backed out of the room to give them some privacy.

I wanted to talk to someone who could tell me about Frank's progress and his status so went to the nurse's station. The supervisor came out from behind the desk with his chart and took us on the side. She told us he was doing well, that he had come through the detox stage of his treatment alright. He was, however, suffering from the early stages of liver disease, but was responding well to the treatments, which included a high-protein diet with a variety of supplements and a combination of pharmaceuticals. Their hope was that with abstinence from alcohol and a proper diet, he could have a full recovery. He was also undergoing psychological evaluation and participating in group therapy to prevent his return to alcohol abuse. They wanted to keep him in the hospital until the end of the year but thereafter he could be treated as an outpatient. I asked if they would consider releasing him on December 24th so that he could be with his family for Christmas. She promised to check with the doctors and let me know.

Well, they had agreed. Jack flew to Portland yesterday, and with a rented a car, picked Frank up and drove him here to Port Orford. We were going to be together for Christmas for the first time since 1941. The long drive afforded them many hours together to bond, both benefitting from the "therapy" of talking about their war experiences and their bouts with alcoholism. Last night, Frank and I sat alone and did our own bonding. He told me he had spoken with his girls several times, that they were being very supportive and had even come to see him again. They were eking out a new relationship, despite his many years of absence from their lives. He was filled with remorse for having lost his wife—their mother—and the ten or so years of his daughters' lives he had missed, and vowed not to miss out on any more. He was ever so grateful to me for saving him, for giving him back his children and his life, and I was glad to have my brother back. I had missed him for so many years. All the times I invited him here for christenings, birthdays, holidays, even when Tom died, I needed him and still he wouldn't come. So, yes, I was happy to have him back in my life.

We were about to sit down to Christmas dinner, when there was a knock on the door. I went to see who it was and shrieked with surprise when I opened the door—it was Jimmy. I threw my arms around him and hugged him tight. "What are you doing here?" I blurted, so stunned. He had gotten leave and hitched a ride with a buddy going to Crescent City. All at once, there was great excitement as the girls and Jack came running to welcome him. Frank was especially thrilled to see him, as he hadn't seen him since he was a baby.

We quickly set another place and sat down to dinner. It was the best Christmas present I could have asked for, to have both my brother and my son home with me. The only thing that could have made me happier was to have Tommy there as well, but I looked around the table at all the happy faces and was grateful. . .and I was optimistic. We had elected a new president who promised to end the war and soon he would step into the office that would allow him to do that. I'd had two letters from Tommy, and he sounded upbeat. He was stationed on the carrier USS *Enterprise* and had settled in to a routine there. He liked his bunk mates and almost made it sound like he was away at camp. He said he was scared that first time he took off and again on the landing, but all his training had kicked in, and he said it was like riding a bicycle, something you never forget, that it was a "piece of cake." He sounded a little cocky to me, but then I knew he was just trying to not add to my worry. I silently said a little prayer that Tommy was alive and well wherever he was, and joined in the merriment at the table.

Port Orford 1970

On my way to work this morning I had stopped in at Beth's Bakery to order a birthday cake for Amy who was about to turn seventeen. It was about 5:30 in the morning, but I knew Beth would be there baking away. Most years I'd just baked my own birthday cakes for my kids, but turning seventeen was somewhat of a rite of passage, warranting a more "official" cake, plus I liked being able to support our local businesses.

Beth was a typical survivor in this town. Her husband had been lost at sea and with young children to raise, she pulled up her boot straps and got creative. She tapped into her talents and started baking cakes, pies and breads for the local businesses right out of her home. Before long, she was able to rent a place with a commercial kitchen and open her own shop selling pastries, breads, espresso and sandwiches to the lunch crowd, in addition to supplying the restaurants like CJ's with rolls and muffins. She now had a thriving business and contributed immensely to this town, as did so many other women. Some widowed, some single, some married, and for whatever reason, they found a safe haven here to start a business and contribute to the community: Like the offbeat studio teaching something called yoga, the flower shop, the pet food store, the cheese shop, a hair salon, realty companies, art studios, an antique store, even the movie theater. It seemed the majority of the businesses were owned by women and I often wondered if that was typical of small towns or unique to Port Orford. In any case, Beth's goods were delicious and she was such fun to be around. I caught up with her for a bit, ordered the cake and got to CJ's just in time to open the door for the day.

Ned was one of my first customers, being his usual bubbly self, filling me in on all the gossip and goings-on in town. He was always a wealth of interesting information and today was no exception. He told me he just heard the Coast Guard station was closing down. . .budget cuts out of Washington he said. It made sense, really. There hadn't been any ships to rescue in years and when small boats got into trouble, they just called out the helicopter from Coos Bay. He said all the men were being relocated and they were planning a decommissioning ceremony for the end of the month.

I was ever so grateful to the Coast Guard for many reasons—not the least of which was saving my son—but especially for having saved Jack and me after the oil line ruptured on his plane and we went down. Were it not for their speedy rescue, who knows if we would have survived. But I also had mixed feelings about our station. True, most of the young men stationed there were well-behaved and respectful. They'd come into CJ's for breakfast and be friendly and nice, talk about where they were from and where they were hoping to go next, anxious to experience new places. But every now and then there'd be a bad apple, an angry young man, a braggart, ready to take on any fight, like that boy Luke who set his sights on my Mary last year. He was from Chicago and far from a model guardsman. He liked to stay out late drinking, and very often came into CJ's early in the morning hung over. He was loud and often rude and flirted with Mary, who of course, thought he was "divine." He was older, handsome and rebellious, and she was flattered by his attention. I was growing concerned, but then, thankfully, he self-destructed in front of her when he came in drunk and acted like a damned fool, having to be dragged outside by his friends. She realized he was bad news and stopped coming into the place to avoid him. Now, he would be leaving, hopefully going somewhere far away.

But in a larger sense, I was sad. That station had been there since I was about 10 years old and was so much a part of this town—heck, the road leading up to the station was called Coast Guard Hill. They'd saved many lives back in the day, including Jack's. Were it not for the brave men of the Coast Guard, he might have been one of those lost at sea. But in the last ten years, with all the advances in technology, there'd been very few rescues, so it stood to reason they would close it down. Especially with all the money that was being wasted on that folly of a war. I asked Ned to let me know when the ceremony would be. . .I surely wanted to attend.

Port Orford 1971

We were living in tumultuous times. The war was dragging on and the nightly news was hard to watch. Horrific scenes of artillery fire, carnage and devastation of a country. We watched quaint villages being burned to the ground with napalm, the inhabitants terrorized, made homeless, many killed or wounded, in order to flesh out hiding Viet Cong or supposed collaborators. We saw whole swaths of jungle being defoliated with chemicals—that couldn't possibly be good to breathe— made brown, dead and ugly. The images were so disturbing, especially seeing bombs being dropped from the air, destroying anything and everything below, and knowing there were, most likely, innocent civilians killed or maimed and that might be my son in that plane dropping the bombs. I had a hard time handling those thoughts and worried for my sons, now both over there, worried not just for their safety, but for their states of mind. Their letters kept coming, but they were mostly inane content. I assumed they didn't want us to know about their getting shot at or possibly even downed and rescued. They didn't know that the media coverage of the war was bringing it into our homes, that we were seeing the anti-aircraft guns firing away, surface-to-air missiles, all the ghastly and seemingly unlimited supply of sophisticated weaponry that was quite successful in bringing down our planes. All of America was watching it, some of it in real time, and they were growing angrier.

There seemed to be just as many protests on the news as the war updates. Then, President Nixon announced the expansion of the war effort into Cambodia, another little country few had ever heard of, and finally, after brewing for month after month, one protest turned deadly. College students at Kent State University in Ohio were protesting the incursion into Cambodia when the crowd grew more hostile. The National Guard was called in and, after an angry confrontation, started shooting, mostly into the air. But when it was over, four students were dead, nine wounded, and the nation was outraged. Soon after, the President announced he would begin both withdrawing troops and negotiations with North Vietnam to end the war. It helped to placate the anger and the violence for a while. Our family even participated in the "Moratorium to End the War in Vietnam" held in Portland. Jack, the girls and I drove to Portland for that one day to march peacefully with thousands of others there and all across the country—even soldiers who had come home—to protest our involvement in Vietnam. And we Americans were not alone, millions joined in cities around the world. For that one day, we were united in our goal, to let our government know we did not approve. But still the war waged on. Every day there were young men, Americans, as well as South Vietnamese, Australians, South Koreans and Thai, dying and coming home terribly wounded; many were being taken prisoner.

Eventually, miraculously, my sons came home, alive, uninjured and seemingly with their psyches intact. But neither boy wanted to talk about the war. I could only imagine what they had seen or experienced. They were back home, out of the conflagration, but they were no longer the boys who anxiously prepared for combat and enthusiastically went off to war. They had lost their innocence, their naiveté. When they first came home and were under my roof, I heard their rustling in the middle of the night. I knew they had nightmares, though they denied it to me, but I knew they confided in each other, so was thankful they had each other to talk to. Tommy did two tours. He wanted to be there while his brother was in the country, even though they never saw each other, were never in the same place at the same time. He came home, was discharged and went to work for Jack. Jimmy did his one tour, then spent his last year at the base in El Centro, California, testing and evaluating aeronautical escape systems. He decided to stay in the Navy, hoping to become an officer, thinking it would improve his chances to become an astronaut, which he still hoped to do.

I continued to marvel at how two boys from the same family could be so different. Tommy liked to fly, but was very much connected to the earth. He loved home and family and the ocean. He soon had a girlfriend and was engaged, he wanted to be tied down. Jimmy, quite the opposite, was never happier than when he was in the air, and especially when he was going fast, breaking speed records, and flying death-defying maneuvers. He loved being a test pilot and resisting gravity. After we and the rest of America watched in amazement the historical events of Apollo 11, he had his sights set on the moon.

With them back on U.S. soil, my thoughts and interests turned to home. Mary was enrolled in Nursing School and was doing well there. She was always a good student, and loved the thought of caring for sick people. I knew she would make a great nurse, if she could stay focused and not get carried away with a boy.

Amy, still in high school, was still active in her anti-pollution campaign and continued to live and breathe every word of Governor McCall. He was an environmentalist and quite vocal and radical in his thinking. His focus was on quality of life for Oregonians. He even made a commercial that welcomed visitors to our cool and clean state, inviting them to come enjoy the beauty and variety of natural environments of our state, to have a great vacation, but ended by saying, "But please don't plan to move here." It was an outrageous thing to say, and thrust us into the national news, but he believed that by limiting the population and development, he could ensure the livability of the state for its citizens for generations to come. He touted our hospitality and created a mystique about the state, one that people did want to see and experience. Little towns like ours thrived on the tourist dollars that flowed through here. As long as Oregonians had jobs and good wages—which they did—they loved him. He was truly a visionary with so many innovative ideas. Amy lived on his every word and even corresponded with him. She wanted to work with him and got a commitment to clerk in his office while she went to Willamette University which was offering a new Environmental Studies program. I was so darned proud of her, of all my kids.

On the home front, life was good and filled with promise. If only the rest of the country and the world could know the peace and hopefulness of a great future that we enjoyed here. Far from the canyons of New York City and the seat of our government in Washington, D.C., we sat glued to the television, in disbelief and a sense of surrealism, as we listened to the reports of the leaked publication of the "Pentagon Papers," which showed the Johnson administration had lied, not only to the American people, but to the Congress, about the depth and breadth of our involvement in the jungles of Southeast Asia. America had been duped. Could we ever trust our government again?

One Saturday, while all this political nonsense was going on, Jack and I were alone and I wanted us to get away from the television and the newspapers and even the pervasive sense of dishonesty that hung in the air, to go someplace out of this world, and I had just the spot. I told Jack to wear some casual clothes and comfortable shoes, we were going for a ride. I grabbed a couple of rain jackets on the way out the door and we headed south in the car but didn't have very far to go. I used to bring the kids here when they were little and they loved it, and so did I. It was a rare and unique experience that would transport us back in time to another place and allow us to forget the woes of the world.

When I saw the sign for the park up ahead, I told Jack to pull in. He looked at me like I was insane and said, "You're kidding, right?"

I assured him I was not and told him it was a special place that he would not believe until he saw it. So, we pulled into Prehistoric Gardens and parked. There were only a few cars in the lot, which made me glad, as we would have the place pretty much to ourselves.

"Jen, I love you, but don't you think this is a little hokey. Looking at a bunch of plastic dinosaurs."

"It's so much more than dinosaurs, and besides, they're not plastic. Come on. I guarantee you will love it." He acquiesced and we got out of the car.

I explained to Jack that this place had opened in 1955 with about a dozen replicas, which is when I had first come. Amy was about two and I had pushed her in a stroller while the others ran around oohing and aahing and shrieking with glee. The man who created it had been a CPA from back east, but was also a sculptor. He moved his family to southern Oregon in search of the perfect place for his park and found this prehistoric rainforest. Over the course of 30 years, he created 23 sculptures, which are steel frames covered by cement, then meticulously hand-painted.

We paid our admission and walked in on the trail following the Dinosaur Traks, all the while Jack was teasing me about having brought him someplace so silly. Greeting us at the trailhead was a Tyrannosaurus Rex, one of the most recognizable and scariest of creatures. This was followed by the largest, a Brachiosaurus, which is 86 feet long and 46 feet tall, and took four years to create. It is spellbinding to stand next to this creature, looking at its huge feet and green hide, as you crane your neck up to see its head. It is huge.

We followed the path and little by little were drawn into the ancient rainforest. It was misting, only adding to the mysteriousness of the place. At each turn, there was a prehistoric reptile lurking, taking us further back into time. It was silent and eerie and so moist, every surface dampened by mist. We forgot about our daily lives and were plunged back to a time when only plants, trees and dinosaurs roamed the earth—it was magical. I looked up at Jack and he looked at me, both of us feeling lost in time. All that moved was the rain dripping off the leaves and ferns of this primitive rainforest. He drew me to him and kissed me in the most tender, loving way. Time stopped for me. All I felt was the warmth of his lips and the beating of our hearts. In that instant, there was only he and I on the whole planet. I felt love for this man that was timeless and infinite. Our spell was broken by the sound of a child shrieking at the sight of the T-Rex. We broke from the kiss but continued to gaze into each other's eyes. He whispered "Thank you" into my ear and I knew he felt the serenity of the forest and that all the nonsense of our daily lives ceased to exist.

We continued on the path discovering and admiring the authenticity and workmanship of these incredible statues, and the raw natural beauty by which we were surrounded, until all too soon we were back at the car. "Thank you" he said again. "I feel so light and free. What a magical place. . .one I would have surely missed if not for you."

"Earlier today, I remembered how transformative this place was for me when I was married to Tom. I could come here with the kids and experience the fun and wonder of the dinosaurs through their eyes. I could forget my unhappiness and just feel the stillness of the forest. I would sit on the bench and close my eyes and imagine I could hear the animals breathing and chewing and running through the ferns in the forest, like they did all those millennia ago. It was cathartic for me and so much fun for the kids. And today, it seemed like just what we needed to change our perspective and realize what truly matters. Us. Just us."

We sat there for a few more moments enjoying the stillness, then continued on down the highway with its incredible panoramic views, without a care in the world, into Gold Beach for a romantic lunch by the sea.

One day, Tommy called me to say he was coming home for a few days; he and his best friends from high school were having a reunion. They'd all been drafted or enlisted after graduation and at last were all home. These four boys had been inseparable in their junior and senior years, and had to put their lives on hold because of that damned war. His friends were so often at our house, they were like sons to me, so I was relieved when each one came home. Like Tommy, Mike wanted to be a pilot, so enlisted in the Air Force. He was sent to Texas for his training and when he was finished, joined a reserve unit there, but luckily, his unit was never called up. He never saw combat, never even left the states.

Larry—who always seemed to have a new girl on his arm and was somewhat cocky and so sure of himself—joined the Marines. He wanted to be "John Wayne," and went off to San Diego for his training. Four months later, he was in South Vietnam at the Khe Sanh Combat Base close to the border with North Vietnam. Not long after arriving there, he was embroiled in almost daily combat, during the Tet offensive, as the Viet Cong tried to destroy or seize the base. It was hard for him to talk about all the killing and about seeing his fellow Marines die beside him. He miraculously made it out alive and relatively unscathed, despite heavy U.S. and allied losses.

And then there was Brad, the most dynamic of the four, whose life adventures would more than fill a whole book. He was either the cleverest of the four or the luckiest. I know he was the heartiest; he loved to surf even in our 50-degree water. Overflowing with personality, he was a sweet kid, but loved to live on the edge. He once told me there wasn't any rule that wasn't meant to be broken or at least bent. And I think it was that thinking, that readiness to bend the rules, that saved him. He waited to be drafted, said they'd have to come get him—he wasn't going willingly. Right after graduation, he went on a road trip, went to visit his father in Arizona (who was long since divorced from his mother) and didn't bother to tell the draft board where he was. That fall, the FBI showed up in town looking for him. One can imagine the stir that created in this sleepy little town when two men in black suits showed up at his mother's house flashing their badges. She was so mad at his father and Brad for leaving, she told the FBI exactly where to find him. As furtively as they arrived, those men were gone. They must have torn up the phone lines from one office to another because in a matter of days, two FBI agents showed up at Brad's door and told him he had two choices: Leavenworth or the Army. In his usual nonchalant way, he said, "I'll take the Army," and that he'd just been waiting for someone to let him know where to go. His carefree attitude must have charmed them because when he said he wanted to get something to eat before going, they took him to lunch before delivering him to the local draft office.

He wound up at an Army base in North Carolina and after claiming his bunk, checked out the base and there discovered a locked building with a swimming pool inside. He went to the office to ask how he could get in to take a swim, that he was a competitive swimmer. The clerk explained that the pool had been closed because there was no lifeguard. Brad told him that he was a trained lifeguard, so could he get in to take a swim. Seems the C.O. heard this conversation and came out of his office to see who this man was. He asked Brad if he was certified and when he said he was—one of those bent rules—the C.O. made him the camp lifeguard and opened the pool. That's where Brad spent his two years of service, lifeguarding at the pool, never once risking his life or even having to rescue a drowning swimmer.

Back together once again, the boys spent three days reconnecting, kicking back, having some fun and trying to forget the two years they'd been robbed of. They showed up at our house Sunday morning for breakfast, ate everything I put on the table and told me their stories. It was so good to see them together, all intact, all having survived that futile war, behaving like the boys they used to be, instead of the men they had been forced to become.

Four young men, four branches of the service and four vastly different stories. The one story I wanted to know, but never heard, was Tommy's. He never wanted to talk about it to me. He told me about his plane, an A-7 Corsair, and what it was like to live on an aircraft carrier, about friends he'd made on the ship, mostly funny anecdotes, but never about the missions he'd flown. I hoped he was talking to someone, like his brother or Jack, to express his feelings about what he'd seen and done. I knew how destructive war could be on the survivors. For now, he seemed well adjusted. . .they all did. And despite the pessimism in the country, these boys were all optimistic about life, anxious to get their lives back on track, and move forward, toward the future.

Port Orford 1987

I just poured myself a cup of coffee and was sitting down to read the *Los Angeles Times* Jack had brought me on Friday. I was feeling pretty dreamy, feeling totally loved and content from having spent the weekend lolling around with him. We didn't do much of anything, both of us tired from the prior week, Jack particularly so. He'd had a rough bout with his intestinal tract, from the ulcers and parasites that continued to plague him all these years later. We'd had the house all to ourselves, with Amy off inspecting a water project all the way up in northeastern Oregon. We sat around watching old movies, talking and napping. The most exercise we got was a short walk on the beach looking for agates. Otherwise, we were two couch potatoes. I remembered being in his arms, in bed, making love, slow and easy. I fell asleep spooned against his long, strong body, feeling his warmth and his breath on my hair.

My mind drifted back to our honeymoon, which was nothing elaborate, but we were alone, with the freedom to explore our minds and bodies. Jack had driven us up the coast to a little village on the cliffs of the sea with a motel of cabins on the beach. In our little cabin, we had all the privacy we needed as we listened to the sounds of the waves crashing on the shore and sea gulls squawking overhead, making love and telling each other our secrets, our hopes and our dreams. There was no room service but all the little cafes and restaurants were willing to deliver food right to our door. In the evenings, we walked on the beach and sat on the sand to watch the sun set over the horizon. It was heavenly, and though we were 20 years younger then, our love was just as passionate today.

I shook myself free of those memories and turned to my coffee and the paper. The headline of the story was "After 42 years, Japanese Heal Forgotten Wound." It was a story about the only U.S. citizens to die on U.S. soil in WWII. I vaguely remembered my father mentioning the incident back in '45 in one of his letters, an explosion of "unannounced cause" that took place east of here on Gearheart Mountain. A minister's wife and 5 children were about to have a picnic when the glade erupted, killing them all. A monument went up on the spot where the explosion occurred and, except for an occasional local newspaper article, the event was forgotten. Years later, it was revealed that the blast was from a Japanese-made balloon bomb. This reminded me of the incendiary bomb that failed in Brookings and the ceremony we had attended during the Azalea Festival. In this case, the article stated, in a convoluted turn of events, a Japanese man who had been held in an internment camp in California, visited Japan and the town where the rice paper was made that was used in the bombs. A woman there told him that, as a young girl, she and her classmates had been removed from school and sent to a factory to make the paper balloons that would carry the bombs. In an effort to express their sorrow, these women had made 1000 origami paper cranes, a symbol of healing and peace, which they asked this Japanese-American man to deliver for them, along with messages to the families of those that died that day on the mountain, all those years ago. It was an amazing story of redemption and forgiveness for all involved parties.

It was bizarre to think of a paper balloon travelling thousands of miles to the interior of Oregon. I was so intrigued, I went to the library to see if I could learn more about these bombs. I found a book that recounted the project with data and information from the Japanese developers of the program. It was fascinating to me. These balloons were large, almost 33 feet in diameter and were made of laminated tissue paper. This paper was primarily made by women from a "cottage industry," women working from home and particularly the teen girls, like the ones who had made the paper cranes for the Gearheart Mountain monument, whose fingers were especially nimble for the task. They made thousands and thousands of sheets of this paper for the estimated six to nine thousand balloons that were ultimately launched. Made of bark that was turned into paper by being beaten, water soaked and kneaded by hand, then assembled and waterproofed with the "fermented juice of green persimmons," these balloons, which were primitively made, were actually very sophisticated in their design and intended use. Fitted with devices to regulate the pressure inside and outside the balloon to carry it thousands of miles during day and night temperatures, a ballast system to keep the balloon flying at 30,000 feet, plus an intricate firing system for the incendiary and high-explosive bombs that were attached, they were anything but primitive devices. In addition to the brilliant technology of the balloon bomb itself, the Japanese had an understanding of air currents, now known as the jet stream, that America knew nothing about.

These balloons were only launched for a six-month period from November of 1944 to April of 1945, the months during which the jet stream was the strongest—meaning the current was strong enough to carry them the thousands of miles to U.S. soil. Coincidently, this period was also winter, a time when most of Canada and the U.S. were moist with rain and snow, which prevented the bombs from wreaking the damage the Japanese sought: forest fires and destruction. Ultimately, there were 297 recorded findings of balloons and their debris in Mexico, Canada and the U.S., 45 in the state of Oregon, and 180 in other states as far east as Michigan. The inventiveness, time, energy, and sheer numbers of people used to make this balloon program happen was to be admired.

The next chapter in this book was about Fujita and his bombing of Brookings, the story of which I knew quite well, which brought me back to thinking about Jack, and how special a man he was. I knew that if it weren't for these incendiary programs being launched by Japanese submarines, I would never have met him, and never would have known the depth of love I felt for and from him.

Reading about these two incidents—Gearheart Mountain and Brookings—made me realize that the Japanese, with their warrior culture, were single-minded in their efforts to bring as much death and destruction to as many of their enemy as possible, but conversely, when not at war, were a calm and peaceful people who sought healing and redemption.

The phone rang; it was Amy calling to say she had to work late again, to go ahead and eat, she would see me later. With no one to cook for, I made myself a cold snack plate and decided to pass the night watching television till Amy got home.

I was sitting in my living room, thinking, "Oh no, not again." The President had just interrupted the show I was watching to announce that he was sending troops into Kuwait to defend them from an Iraqi incursion. Once again, we were at war, risking the lives of American men—and now women—to defend some little country that most of us didn't know where it was located. I knew it was in the Middle East, but where exactly, I couldn't tell you. War. It was still hard for me to comprehend. I understood that when you or someone you love is threatened you have to fight back. I get that. I understood World War II. We were attacked, on American soil, so we had to fight back. But the rest of the wars were not so easy to digest. Was a human life so invaluable, that a government cared little if it was sacrificed? Or was it that being a citizen meant being willing to sacrifice one's life for country? Did the men who sat behind closed doors in the White House deciding to go to war and how many men to direct, were they ready to send their own sons into combat? Had they ever seen combat, been in it, been fired on, bombed, at risk of losing life or limb? Did they stop to think of the troops as people, boys and girls really, with families—parents or spouses and children of their own—or were they just pawns, collateral, part of the cost of waging war?

I knew I was viewing this all too simplistically, but I had seen the casualties of war: The torn-up bodies, filled with shrapnel, burns, bullet wounds, missing arms, legs, hands; the skeletal bodies from the camps, covered in sores and scars from the many beatings they suffered, sick with malaria, dysentery, all kinds of parasites. I'd also perceived the scars you couldn't see, the psychological wounds that would plague their victims for years to come or perhaps the rest of their lives, with alcoholism, drug abuse, homelessness. I'd seen many of the thousands of flag-draped caskets and knew, worst of all, there were so many who never came home, leaving families forever wondering where or how they fell. The expression that "War is Hell," is so true, but hearing that, do we fathom the depth of the brutality, the barbarism, the atrocities that are committed, the horrifying scenes of destruction, not only of buildings and landscapes, but of bodies blown to bits? The combat during the war was only a part of the horror. When soldiers came home, they were faced with new challenges, new fights to be won. When the anti-war public sentiment was strong, as it was during the Vietnam war, our brave soldiers came home to expressions of disdain and revulsion instead of the respect and honor they deserved. But perhaps the ultimate betrayal for veterans, who willingly risked their lives when their government asked, was making them fight to prove their sicknesses and disabilities were actually caused by the war in order to receive the free medical treatment they needed, or to be compensated. These were the worst indignities of war. And nowhere during or after the fact, when casualties were calculated, were the men counted who died at young ages after serving in the war. Men, particularly those held prisoner, like my Jack, who didn't make it to 70 or much beyond, due to their afflictions.

I know I am far too idealistic to think that there is an alternative to war. With the incredible advances we have made in this century—putting men on the moon and living in space, computers, mobile phones, supersonic planes—you would think some alternative to the mass destruction could be found. Or was there some loftier way of thinking that war is good. It's true that during WWII, here in this country where war was thousands of miles away and there was no real threat of bombs dropping on us or of being invaded by hostile troops, people felt pride and a great sense of patriotism. They had jobs where previously none existed; they were united toward a shared goal, and were willing to make necessary sacrifices if it was for the good of our troops. There was comradery and incredible innovation in materials and processes, that would ultimately benefit man and manufacturing. But in my mind, to my way of thinking, that "good" didn't come anywhere close to outweighing the "bad."

I knew I was just being naïve and that my emotions were still raw. Wars have been fought throughout the centuries, on all continents. Whenever a territory or resources were threatened or encroached upon, there was a fight. And the size of each side's might and willingness to pursue the prize determined whether it was one fight or a war. Like here, in little Port Orford. When Captain Tichenor's men came ashore to claim the land for a settlement in 1851, their superior weapons overpowered the Native Americans who had lived here for hundreds, or perhaps thousands, of years. If it weren't for that particular land grab, I wouldn't be sitting here today.

I knew my thinking—my great love of peace—came from living where I did, albeit a place born out of a fight, but a place where there is plenty of space. Our population was so small, everyone had plenty of room and there were enough resources for everyone's needs. We were isolated, living out on the fringe, with limited accessibility, and surrounded by nature: forests, mountains, rivers, farms, an ocean and wildlife. I could look out my window at a female deer and her new baby grazing on my grass. Yesterday, she was pregnant and now here, miraculously, was this cute little creature, barely a foot high, covered in spots, romping after her and chewing grass right beside her. I look beyond them at the ocean and there's a whale spout, from a migrant gray whale passing through, or just look at the yard, a sea of yellow dandelions dancing in the wind, with the silvery ocean and rugged tree-covered, green mountains beyond. It's idyllic. Our only enemy here is the forces of nature, which we know all too well can be destructive: the storms with howling winds, flooding rain and high seas; the potential threat of tsunami or earthquake or volcanic eruption, like when Mt. St. Helens blew her top, not so very far from here.

For almost 20 years, our country had known peace, or more accurately, was not at war. After that last helicopter flew out of Saigon in '75 and the national upheaval of Watergate, governmental corruption and the resignation of a Vice-President and a President, the country simmered down. The Iranian hostage crisis, though a horrifying experience for the 52 hostages and their families, actually did more to heal our wounds. Our country was united in solidarity toward a common goal: to bring our fellow Americans home. We sent cards and letters to the hostages, to let them know they were not forgotten, and yellow ribbons blew from trees and posts in every town, including this one. Most were shredded and faded when, after 444 days, the hostages finally came home.

But here we were putting boots on the ground again. My only hope was that it would be quick and the casualties low. I was thankful my sons had completed their military obligation and that my only grandchildren were girls. I couldn't bear to sacrifice any more people I loved. Jack was gone for almost a year and I still missed him every day; the big hole he left in my heart was still there. I remember the day Jack called me about five years ago, when his intestinal bouts started becoming more frequent. He was thinking about leaving LA and coming to live with me and he wanted to know if I would be alright with that. Needless to say, I was more than alright with it, I was thrilled. I told him I thought it was a great idea, that no doubt the stress of his business and the pollution of that city was taking its toll on him. He wondered though how he would fill his time and not get on my nerves. I suggested he could open an organic food store or a juice bar, that the things that were good for him would be good for others; or with all the fertile land around here, he could start an organic farm. He got so excited by these ideas, it took him less than a week to close up his life in LA, legally turning over the business and his house to Tommy, and saying goodbye to friends. He showed up here with two suitcases and overflowing enthusiasm to start this new phase of his life with new ventures. He started in right away hiring excavators and carpenters to clear the lower field on this big property and put up several large greenhouses where he grew all kinds of vegetables, especially greens which he used in the smoothies he sold in a little storefront he rented in the middle of town and named "Juicing Jack's." He was a man on a mission, so got together with other locals and was instrumental in the opening of a food coop where healthy organic foods could be available to the whole community. In the process of generating healthy food for himself and the town, he employed quite a few locals who needed the work, so he didn't have to be consumed with work or stress, which he certainly didn't need. He thrived for a while; his health improved and he grew strong again. He loved being close to the earth and he saw he was really making a difference in so many people's lives. And, of course, I fussed over him and nurtured him in ways he'd never known, having been on his own for the better part of his life.

But then his health started to decline, no matter how much I pampered him or how healthily he ate. He was the first person I knew who ate organic food, took probiotics, ate a macrobiotic diet—things I had never heard of before—and drank smoothies, long before they ever had that name. He did a great deal of research about holistic healing, and knew more than most about food and nutrition because his stomach and intestines were fragile from his time in the camps, but over time, the problems became unmanageable. The long period of starvation and dysentery did irreparable damage to his digestive system and other organs. He grew thinner, frailer, his body unable to absorb nutrients. He was in and out of the hospital, had numerous surgeries. The last time, he was so weak, he caught pneumonia and died in my arms. I watched the light go out of his beautiful blue eyes, taking the spark of my life with it. He was the love of my life. He had my heart and when he died, half of me died with him. I was alive, I was breathing, but I was just going through the motions of life, for my kids and my grandchildren. They were all that brought me any happiness at all, particularly Mary's latest baby. She was especially precious to me because she was born the night Jack died—one door had closed and another opened. Mary named her Jacqueline, Jackie for short, and she was a very energetic, happy child with beautiful blue eyes, just like Jack's. I was just sad that Jack never got to see her.

I heard Amy calling my name, she had just walked in the door. "In here," I called back to her. If it weren't for Amy who still lived with me, I am not sure I would still be alive today. I might have just been content to sit here and wither away, with the thought of being with Jack once again. She made sure I ate and exercised, got up every day and dressed. She travelled a lot, working for the DEQ, where she'd worked for many years, getting her start from Governor McCall, who had created that agency and gave her an entry management position. She now headed that agency and spent much of her time in her office in Salem, as well as visiting hot spots and new environmental projects all around the state, but made sure she was home at least every weekend. I told her not to bother, but she insisted this was where she wanted to be, this was still her home.

I asked her once why she hadn't married and she told me it was because she had yet to meet a man like Jack. I was stunned when she said that, but she explained that though she was young, she remembered what home was like when her father was still alive. She remembered how Tom and I acted together, what our family life was like with him. That became her benchmark for marriage. But when Jack entered our life, it was all so different, that there was a dynamic shift in our family. She saw how much happier I was and how much happier the whole family was with him. She felt life was far more interesting and fun with him around. She decided that if she couldn't feel for a man what she could see I felt for Jack, to have that depth of love and respect that she saw we shared, she didn't want to settle for something less, and she was okay with that. She said her life was quite full and rich with friends, siblings and nieces, and the work she was doing was very fulfilling. For now. I was glad she said "for now," because I hoped the day would still come when she would meet a man and know the kind of love I had known with dear, sweet Jack.

"Are you ready, Mom?" she asked me.

"Yes, I'm dressed and ready." She was taking me to a doctor's appointment, insisting my lethargy and lack of appetite was not normal, even for someone grieving as I still was. I didn't agree with her, but she wouldn't take no for an answer, so I agreed to go. She handed me my purse, and we were out the door.

Port Orford 1992

 I stopped on the trail to take in the view, which I never tired of. All I could see was blue in the glimmering sunlight, between the sea and the sky, so many different shades—an hombre of blues, including the clearest pure blue that reminded me of Jack's eyes. I knew he was beaming down on me from wherever he was: the great beyond, the hereafter, an alternate dimension, the next life, wherever one goes when the body dies. At that moment, I felt enveloped by his love and such joy in knowing he was free from all his earthly suffering. Looking at the ocean with its roiling kinetic energy, I was reminded of impermanence, that teaching of Thich Nhat Hanh stayed with me and helped me to accept whatever loss came my way. Nothing stays the same, it is always different, like the spot I was standing and the ocean in my view. I saw a wave forming out of a swell. It was see-through and teal blue. Its lip curled and rolled all the way down the line. I could feel its intense power as it crashed down on itself and became white foam that poured around and over the rocks, creating mini waterfalls, the water returning back into the sea, only to be sucked out into a swell and start all over again. But it was always different, from moment to moment. Different years, different seasons, different days. The light, the sun, the wind, the clouds, the terrain was always different. I thought of the many thousands of times I had hiked these Heads since it became a state park in the early 70's and it was never the same. The changes might be imperceptible to most observers, but they were there. Just as it was with people. From the moment of our birth, our entrance into the living world as an embodied soul, until our heart stops beating and we pass into that next place, each moment is different. I knew that soon my heart, which was so full of love, would cease to beat and my being, my essence, my soul, whatever we wish to call it, would pass on to whatever came next.

But for today, for this moment, I had gratitude, for this place, so desolate and serene, where I seemed to be the only person in existence, where I could walk in silence and tranquility, alone with my thoughts, amongst the scrubby bushes, the wind-bent trees, the hearty little flowers and buds that survived despite the harshness of the environment. Often plied with wind, rain, and frigid air, they clung to life and waited for the sun to kiss them and the wind to mellow to a gentle breeze, when they could prosper for me to appreciate and remark upon. I was grateful for a still-strong body to carry me along the trail and for the senses to enjoy every single aspect, to touch the flora, to smell the air, to see beauty in even a termite-eaten, downed tree, to hear the chirps and cries of the indigenous and migrating birds, and to feel the shock as the sea violently crashed into the continent's rugged edge.

I stood now at the northernmost point on the trail and looked north, past the miles of uninhabited beach to the Cape and the Lighthouse. Except for the fence that prohibited me from walking further onto a risky precipice, if I had stood here a hundred years ago, the view would have been virtually the same. Perhaps the trees would have been smaller or less bent, the beach might have been thinner or wider, the rocks less eroded. But this was one place I could feel timeless, a place where it seemed time stood still. Untouched by developers, resorts, fast-food restaurants and golf courses, a last frontier to be enjoyed by my children and their children and hopefully, many generations to come.

I remembered my parents then, how loving and committed they were, to each other and to Frank and me. They wanted us to have rich childhoods filled with wonder and adventure and a great deal of independence. They taught us to make good decisions, to be honest and to always try to do the right thing. That made me think of Tom and my decision to marry him. In many ways, it was a bad decision. . . he made me feel unloved and robbed me of my independence, two cherished things my parents bestowed upon me. But he gave me four beautiful children that I loved with all my heart, who enriched my life in ways I never could have dreamed, from the very moment they were born. I felt sorrow for the man, whose life could have been so much more, so much fuller and no doubt much longer.

I walked along the well-trodden path as I contemplated these things, and found myself at our bench—Jack's and my bench—where we sat holding each other for so many hours watching the sea and the whales, and breath-taking sunsets, and I smiled. I sat and once again was filled with gratitude, for the many years I had with him and all the love he showered upon me and my children, and for the way he helped shape their lives. Looking at the vista before me, devoid of people, machines or man-made structures, I remembered the summer Jack suggested we try living in Los Angeles. As soon as school let out, we packed up the kids and closed up the house and moved to Jack's house outside the city. The kids learned to play tennis and enjoyed swimming in the pool, but missed their friends and the ability to just run down the hill to the beach or the park for hours of carefree fun and exploration. At Jack's, they needed to be driven if they wanted to go anywhere, even the movies, which they normally walked to. There were so many people and so many cars and I started to have fear that they would get hurt or taken advantage of in some way. I was afraid to let them out of my sight and could feel myself withering, and so, was thrilled when one day in August Jack told me how much he missed Port Orford, the clean air, the space, the ease of life. Within the week, we were back at our home—the last frontier—safe and free to roam, returned to the pastoral way of life we had enjoyed before leaving.

I took a deep breath and noticed a few gray clouds moving toward me from the northwest and decided to move on. I savored my surroundings for another moment, then continued on the path, mindful of each step, coming to the place where the watch tower once had been, when this was a U.S. Coast Guard station. There again I stopped and tried to envision it, to remember the young men who served here, risking their lives to save others, and imagined them, hearts pounding, as they ran along the path and up the steps to search for ships in distress off the sometimes-treacherous coast. I looked down at my feet, feeling the energy of the molten earth thousands of feet below, realizing then all the history that was steeped into this very earth, and that I was connected to it and to those men and the many thousands of hikers who explored this trail before this day. I hoped that at least some of them appreciated its beauty and took the time to read the storyboards to learn its past as I did, to learn that at the end of the last glacial age, some 11,000 years ago, the warming climate melted the ice caps which raised the sea level, creating a western coastline further inland. I stood looking out to the horizon, from my perch on this rocky promontory, surrounded by ocean on three sides, trying to imagine a coastline that once stood many miles west of here.

The clouds were coming closer and growing darker, so I continued on around the back side, through the tunnel of trees, past the last of the time-worn "fingers" that create this headland. I heard the sea gulls cry as I walked along the trail, past Nellie's Cove, stopping once more at the overlook, to look down upon the place where the boathouse once stood, that contained the lifeboat that would carry the men out for dangerous rescues at sea. All of it gone now, except for the photos that hung in the Museum, once the living quarters for the brave men stationed here, where I had spent countless hours reading their letters, looking at their photos, surveying the myriad of artifacts that documented their existence.

I heard the rumble of distant thunder and decided it was time to go. I trudged on up the hill on the last bit of the trail, past the Museum and the refurbished lifeboat on display as the sky darkened. I got to the parking lot, filled with vehicles, and into my car. Just as I closed the door, the skies opened and drenched the earth where moments before I stood. As I let my car warm a bit, I noticed a half dozen people dashing from the trees, making for their cars. I was glad to see that others were drawn to the nature, to the geologic wonder that is the Port Orford Heads. Feeling a bit tired but quite relaxed, I put my car in gear for the drive down the hill to home, where Amy would be waiting for me and wondering where I was.

Epilogue

I was looking around the room at my family, all together at the same time, which was rare, though for a not-so-happy occasion. Tommy was here with his wife and three girls, all beautiful teenagers, one just starting college and the other two right behind. He was really happy. His business was successful and had expanded several times over the years, from when he first started working for Jack in that little charter flight company. The business now included a flight school, which is where he spent most of his time, teaching would-be pilots how to fly. He hired pilots to fly the charters, as he still hated to be away from home. He lived outside of LA, in Jack's old house, up a canyon, where he was surrounded by mountains and trees, far from the sounds of the city. Here, they were staying in one of the duplexes of the motel below us, planning to stay a few days.

Jimmy was here too but couldn't stay. He was a Lieutenant Commander of a ship somewhere in the Pacific, based out of Pearl Harbor. He had gotten flown off the ship back to Oahu, then took a commercial flight to get here for the occasion. His wife was a beautiful Hawaiian woman and was about to give birth to his first child, so had stayed behind. When I first saw him yesterday, I remembered the little boy who wanted to become an astronaut. His life had not taken that path, but here he was a mature man, looking ever so distinguished in his uniform, tall and trim with a few gray hairs visible beneath the brim of his cap, a career Naval officer, a Commander of men and a colossally huge ship.

Mary was chasing her 2-year-old daughter who had wriggled out of the car and was about to run into the roadway.

She was beautiful as ever but was being worn out by this rambunctious little girl. She was a late-in-life baby, a surprise. Mary was 39 when she came along, thinking she was done having children, after her first two, now 12 and 14. She seemed content, but I'm not sure Mary was entirely satisfied with how her life turned out, though she seemed happy enough with her family. She had a great husband with whom she wanted for nothing, but I sensed that she had envisioned a more exotic, glamourous life than that of a suburban homemaker in Oregon.

It was time to start the service. We were gathered around the gravesite about to bury the most important member of our family. We were all pretty broken up about her death, her having died so quickly and so young. I was feeling the loss so much greater than the others because I'd spent so much more time with her. We'd lived together far longer than any of the others. We were not just mother and daughter, but best friends, confidants. I was not looking forward to life without her. I heard the minister speaking but was lost in my memories. All those tender, unforgettable moments that occur between a mother and her last-born child. I thought of Mary and Jackie and wondered if they would have the same, special relationship.

I looked over at the other side of the gathering. There were many people there, come to pay tribute to her. Some faces I recognized and many I didn't. These were people who knew her from the many phases of her life, each knowing a small part of her, in a different time and a different place. But it was safe to say, she was special to them for them to have come all this way.

When the minister was finished, it was time to leave. We were asked to bid our final farewell. I was the last one remaining at her side and felt my feet glued to the earth. I didn't want to leave her; I didn't want to say goodbye. I'm not sure how long I stood there, tears streaming down my face, wanting to feel her arms around my shoulders, her kiss upon my forehead. Then, Jimmy was by my side, his arm around me, urging me away. He said, "She's not in that box. She's in your heart, always." I knew he was right and squeezed his arm as he led me away.

Back at the house, I had a chance to talk with many of her friends and listen to their stories of how they knew her and the impact she had had on their lives. She'd always been special to us, her family, but to hear the gratitude from strangers, gave her life far more meaning. Each person I spoke with added another piece of the puzzle that was her life. By the time the last guest left, I was bursting with pride.

Mary was gathering her things, getting ready to leave. I said to her and her brothers, "Wait. Before you all leave, I want to show you something." I went to my room to retrieve the leather folio I had found. It was thick and bursting with loose sheets of paper of all different sizes and colors. I held it out for them to see and told them, "I found this when I was looking for her burial clothes. It's a journal of sorts. Stories of her life, going as far back as when she was a young girl." Tommy came over and took it from me and started to thumb through it. "I've read the whole thing. We're all in it and it does contain secrets and intimacies, but it is beautifully written with a fresh and innocent voice. I was thinking I'd like to publish it. If you have no objections." They were all gathered around it now, reading over each other's shoulders.

"I think other people would love to read it because so much of it is about this town and its history. She's painted an enthralling picture of life in a small town from a native's point of view." They started taking pages out of it, reading it and passing it around. I hoped I would be able to put it back in order. They were reading and chatting, commenting on various events, so I left them to go clean up in the kitchen. After a while, Tommy called me back into the living room.

"We think you're right, this will make a great book. What do you think the title should be?" Tommy asked.

"Well, I was thinking of 'The Rescue,' since that's when her writing started, or 'War and Peace on the Oregon Coast.' Or perhaps, we should just call it 'The Memoir of Jennifer Long.'"

I wanted the world to know my mother's story. True, she was a tiny cog on a giant wheel, but her life mattered. She made a difference in so many people's lives. She was not formally educated, but was incredibly smart and knowledgeable. She was not worldly or well-traveled, but her lessons learned from life in a small town were universal. She was not politically savvy, but knew that war was inhumane and its destruction was felt in uncountable ways long after the peace agreement was signed. She was not religious, but was more kind, more charitable than most church-goers. And she understood that no matter where you lived, big city or small village, in this country or another, thousands of miles away, we are all connected, that we must care for each other, have respect for one another, save each other if we can, and the most important thing in life is family. I was sorry if the events in this book were out of order, I tried my best to put it back together in a way that made sense.

But the words are hers, a narrative diary of her life, except for two stories she did not get to write. At her funeral, the minister was her brother, Frank. He spoke of how she had saved him—from himself, his guilt, and the alcohol that would have surely killed him. She allowed him to redeem himself, in his own eyes and also the eyes of his daughters and the Lord. After he completed the rehab that she had fought so hard to get him into, he realized that only with the help of a higher power could he stay the course. With her help and her guidance, he had become a minister. He now led a small congregation in a small town not far from Portland, and sponsored a small shelter for homeless veterans struggling with addiction. She had inspired him to "give back," to make a difference in people's lives. She had made him more than he ever dreamed he could be and he hoped she would have been proud of him.

Those words rang so true, for I knew she had done that with every one of us. That was my mother, the rescuer. Jack always said she had saved him, as did her friend Sam, and I knew she had saved Tommy, Jimmy, Mary and me from countless tragedies and lives spent in risky, hard jobs.

The other story she could not have written was about her own funeral, and the more than hundred people who came to honor her. Sam was there with a few other men around the same age as him, who I found out later were men who had come through the hospital ward where my mother worked all those years ago, during the war. Of course, there was Ned and a few other local widowers who swore my mother saved them from utter despair with her kindness and friendship. She brought them casseroles and invited them to dinner at our house on the holidays, not wanting them to be alone. The rest were women from this town, women who had lost their husbands and fathers of their children to the sea or to the forest. The wives of fishermen and loggers who my mother had helped with food, clothing and money she often couldn't spare. They were grateful for the countless collection jars she had placed at CJ's, and when filled with customer's loose change and her own tips, she delivered selflessly to these women then struggling to feed and clothe the children left behind. Some she supported for a week, and some for months, till they could resettle with family or friends or find a job or start a business. That was my mother, always thinking of someone less fortunate than herself. They had all come to pay tribute to her memory. She had truly left her mark in this life and this town that she loved, this "last frontier of the fading west" as she liked to call it.

Author's Note

Though many of the characters are inspired by actual residents of Port Orford, all of them are fictional, with two exceptions: Governor Tom McCall and Nobuo Fujita.

Many of the events recounted in these pages actually occurred, such as the sinking of the *Larry Doheny,* on October 5, 1942, by a Japanese submarine just off the coast, with survivors being brought to Port Orford. The bombing outside of Brookings by Nobuo Fujita in 1942 and his subsequent ceremonial return twenty years later are well documented, as are the Columbus Day Storm of 1962, and the explosion on Gearheart Mountain (see Mitchell Recreation Area on Wikipedia for more information). The Port Orford Meteorite is a true myth or hoax, somewhat famous around the area.

The Prehistoric Gardens is a tourist attraction on Highway 101 south of Port Orford, and the Cape Blanco Lighthouse is the oldest, continuously-operating light in Oregon, receiving thousands of visitors each year. The Port Orford Heads, a state park on the site of the former U.S. Coast Guard Station, is a local attraction offering hiking trails and a Museum.

Acknowledgements

Though this book is fictional, I wanted it to be historically accurate and to that end, I would like to acknowledge a few of the wonderful books I read: As background for World War II and POW's: <u>Baa Baa Black Sheep</u> by Pappy Boyington, <u>My Hitch in Hell</u> by Lester I. Tenney, <u>Prisoners of the Japanese</u> by Gavin Daws, and <u>They Also Served: American Women in World War II</u> by Olga Gruhzit-Hoyt. About the balloon bombs and Nobuo Fujita's bombing on Brookings: <u>Silent Siege. Japanese Attacks Against North America in World War II</u> by Bert Webber. For much of the history and flavor of Port Orford: <u>Fool's Hill</u> by John Quick, <u>Port Orford. A History</u> by Patrick Masterson and <u>Port Orford and North Curry County</u> by Shirley Nelson.

The title for this book is a line borrowed from the poem, "Curry County" by the late Frances Haelstrom, a beautiful descriptor of this place.

I am grateful to the many people of Port Orford who welcomed me and told me stories, much of which became content or inspired characters. Especially, Brad Pease, who became a friend and enthralled me with the many twists and turns of his life; Kate King-Van Wormer, another friend and the owner of Tasty Kate's, a warm and friendly café that allowed me to sit and eavesdrop on many interesting conversations; Rockne Berge, who suggested many topics worth researching and introduced me to Owen Miller, who shared his war memorabilia. To Tim Palmer, a prolific local author, who gave me invaluable advice. To Ernie Thayer, who always encouraged me to keep writing, even when I was stuck. And most especially, Russ Gibson, the owner of this house—the old Port

Authority Building—where the idea for this book and its characters came to me, and have sat for over a year, writing away.

Thanks to my friends Mark Zunic and Stephanie Hartung who graciously read chapters for me and offered helpful feedback.

Special thanks to my friend Ui Goldsberry, author of several books, including the <u>Pocket Guide to the Hawaiian Islands</u>, for her invaluable advice, encouragement and direction. And to her author-husband Steven Goldsberry, who gifted me with his <u>The Writer's Book of Wisdom</u>, a powerhouse of a little book which made me a better (I hope) writer.

Most importantly, eternal gratitude to my husband Cory, who gave me the place and the quiet I needed to focus on writing, who believed in my ability and supported my efforts to make this crazy idea for a book a reality.

66661446R00141

Made in the USA
Lexington, KY
20 August 2017